IN THE STREETZ 5

A King's Game

TRON HILL

URBAN AINT DEAD PRESENTS

URBAN AINT DEAD

P.O Box 448

Maybrook, NY 12543

SOUNDTRACKS

Scan the QR Code below to listen to the Soundtracks/Singles of some
of your favorite U.A.D titles:

Don't have Spotify or Apple Music?
No Sweat!
Visit your choice streaming platform and search URBAN AINT
DEAD.

Currently on lock serving a bid?
JPay, iHeartRadio, WHATEVER!
We got you covered.
Simply log into your facility's kiosk or tablet, go to music and search
URBAN AINT DEAD.

URBAN AINT DEAD PRESENTS

Like & Follow us on social media:

FB - URBAN AINT DEAD

IG: @uadpresents

Tik Tok - @uadpresents

Submission Guidelines

Submit the first three chapters of your completed manuscript to urbanaintdead@gmail.com, subject line: Your book's title. The manuscript must be in a .doc file and sent as an attachment. The document should be in Times New Roman, double-spaced, and in size 12 font. Also, provide your synopsis and full contact information. If sending multiple submissions, they must each be in a separate email. Have a story but no way to submit it electronically? You can still submit to URBAN AINT DEAD. Send in the first three chapters, written or typed, of your completed manuscript to:

URBAN AINT DEAD
P.O Box 448
Maybrook, NY 12543

DO NOT send original manuscript. Must be a duplicate.
Provide your synopsis and a cover letter containing your full contact information.
Thanks for considering URBAN AINT DEAD.

CHAPTER ONE

Ace

"What the fuck am I doing?" Another tear streaked his face. He let the pistol fall away from his hand onto the passenger seat.

How could he have reached such a stage in life where he was ready to take his own? Never had he even contemplated doing such a thing. But then again, never had he been under so much pressure. Shit was the worst, and he'd lost his best friend.

Ace massaged the bridge of his nose, feeling as though a headache was right outside his brain's door, patiently waiting to be let in. He reached for the blunt and lighter. In that very instance, a dark object tugged for his attention at the corner of his eye. Slowly, his head turned, catching sight of a dark SUV completing its creep on the side of his car.

There was nothing about the vehicle that he could make out besides the protruding muzzle aiming from the passenger's window – and then the face of a ghost behind it.

"Fuc…"

Pop! Pop! Pop!

The loud popping alerted all of Ace's senses, pulling him back to the last scene he remembered – or thought he did.

Instinctively, his body jerked sideways over the console, hoping to avert any fatal bullets. His hand covered his head protectively as his heart pounded against his ribcage. His breaths came shallow, each one feeling like it could be his last. He braced himself for the inevitable – but nothing happened. The only sound was a voice shouting from outside the car door.

"Put your fucking hands where I can see them!"

Ace hadn't thought to open his eyes. Preventing as much damage as possible was his first priority. Everything else – secondary. He remained motionless, body tensed, while the person on the other side of the door continued to shout commands. Ace didn't have to guess who it was; only one set of people used those type of words. *Fuck!*

Parting his eyelids, Ace could see the luminous rays protrude around him. How did he stir from one nightmare into another? His mind quickly treaded over a few scenarios as his gaze settled on the assault rifle beneath him on the passenger seat. The officer had a flashlight aimed at him and most likely a gun too. He would be killed before he even attempted to lift the choppa.

"Raise your hands where I can see them!" the man screamed again. After another moment, Ace began to slowly comply, squinting his eyes. "Keep your hands in my sight." The officer moved closer, snatching on the door handle. The door was locked.

Ace heard the man's feet shuffle on the concrete.

"Slowly use your left hand to unlock the doors, sir." The officer's voice was steady, but Ace could sense the caution behind it. Most likely, he had already spotted the rifle on the passenger seat and wasn't taking any chances. Ace would have to put him at ease because if he didn't, not even a small pinch of a chance to escape would be presented.

"Don't shoot me, man. I'm not resisting!" Ace yelled. Doing as instructed, he unlocked the doors. The feet shuffled again before the door was yanked open. "What's all this…"

"Step out of the vehicle and keep your hands where I can see them."

"Ight, can you get that flashlight out of my face, damn?" Ace said, placing his sight on the pavement beneath his feet. For the first time he noticed the rapid flashes of the cruiser's strobe lights. Standing, the man ordered him to place his hands on the roof, which he did. The officer's hand frantically searched what it could while the other pushed the barrel of the gun into his back.

Swiftly, Ace looked up and down the street, suddenly becoming grateful. He knew that at some point, the officer would have to holster the weapon to place cuffs on him. This would create a small window of opportunity for him. And the clear street made that window expand a bit more.

Finally, the man's hand stopped. Ace took it as his cue. "Officer, can you tell me what's going on, man? I haven't done nothing wrong to be getting arrested."

"Sir, why were you sleeping in a parked car with an assault rifle on the seat?" As Ace answered, the officer began chatting codes into his walkie-talkie. The gun hadn't moved yet.

"Honestly," Ace began, "I didn't know I fell to sleep. But I have a license for the rifle in the glove compartment if you'd…"

"I'll check it out. But right now, I'm going to place you in the backseat of my cruisier for my safety, okay?"

"Okay, I'm cool with that," Ace told him. He could feel the man's trembling hand grip the back of his neck as the gun left his back. Ace waited until he heard the removal of the handcuffs.

"Sir, bring your right arm down first."

Hastily, Ace brought the left one down. "Sir, I said…" In one swift motion, Ace threw his right elbow back with force, pivoting his entire body backwards into the officer's. His elbow had connected with the officer's jaw, causing him to instinctively duck away.

Without any hesitation, Ace swung at the man who was now the biggest threat to his freedom. He knew he'd have a minimal timeframe before his backup came. Every action counted now because every second meant either life or death.

His fist crashed into the officer's forehead, causing him to stumble farther backwards. Desperately, the officer's hand went for his holster, fingers fumbling at the butt of the gun. But Ace was faster.

Rushing him to the ground, Ace gripped the man's wrist, pinning both hand and gun down. The officer struggled, his eyes bulging wide with fear, as his free hand pushed against Ace's face. Shaking his head loose from the hand, Ace delivered a brutal punch to the man's face then another one which hit him in the temple.

Ace could feel that the last blow had weakened the officer's resistance. Quickly, he threw another hard right to seize the moment. Dazed and defeated, the man's head fell backwards. Ace yanked the man's wrist upward and twisted it, prying the gun away from his grasp. He was now in control. Weakly, the officer reached, causing Ace to slap the arm away and slam the butt of the gun into the his cranium.

Quickly getting to his feet, Ace swept his eyes over the scene. Nothing had changed except for the officer lying motionless in the middle of the street. Then there were approaching headlights cutting through the night.

Without hesitation, he took a few steps and hopped into the car, turning over the ignition. The engine growled to life just as the oncoming vehicle neared. In a matter of seconds, the driver would see the officer sprawled in the road but not before spotting him slipping away into the darkness.

Ace clenched his jaw, gripping the wheel. Both occurrences would set off a chain reaction, another small window for him to jump through.

Caring less at this point, Ace pressed down hard on the accelerator, causing the rental to rapidly lurch forward. Time was definitely of the essence. He needed to find another car before the description of this one made it across the airwaves to every policeman within this vicinity.

As he passed the vehicle, Ace kept his eyes on the rearview mirror, watching until its taillights flared red. Without hesitation, he eased off the gas, making a sharp left onto the next street.

His gaze darted between the road and the unfamiliar surroundings. The night swallowed most of the details, leaving him a bit confused. He had no idea where he was. The lack of bright streetlights and recognizable landmarks made it impossible to get his bearings.

However, one thing was certain. He was still in DeKalb County. The officer's uniform had told him that much.

Driving, Ace's mind rewound back to something he'd remembered before the cop woke him. Whiteboy had called. His voice had been strained, telling Ace he'd been shot.

Ace had rushed to the Holiday Inn Express where Whiteboy had been staying. Now, he remembered the police presence, the flashing lights, the swarm of uniforms. He had been too late.

Then, there was the gurney, the lifeless body covered in a sheet. *Fuck!!!*

Instantly, Ace slammed his foot on the brakes, causing the tires to scream loudly as he unintentionally made a screeching right. The car would only go a few more feet before he brought it to a complete stop.

"Fuck, fuck, fuck!!!" he yelled, hitting the steering wheel. *That couldn't of been White, man,* he told himself, looking aimlessly beyond the windshield. Then, a sudden thought came to mind.

Frantically, Ace lifted the rifle and began searching the seat, then around the console, until his hand felt what he was looking for on the floor. Bringing the phone's screen alive, he quickly found Whiteboy's number and called. After three rings, the call was forwarded to his voicemail. He called again and got the voicemail a second time.

"Fuck!" Ace growled, mindlessly throwing the phone into the windshield, shattering it into pieces. Tears began to mount in the corners of his eyes as the realization of the situation set in. His best friend was gone.

Ace placed his head against the steering wheel, letting the streams of his pain run freely from the web of his eyes. His brother had been ripped away from his life without warning. The raw ache in his chest grew with each passing second. Memories of their yesterdays flashed through his mind – everything from their shared laughter to the late nights and all the moments that had defined their bond. Now, it was all just… gone.

Ace squeezed the steering wheel until his knuckles turned white, his breaths coming in ragged gasps. The car felt like a prison, trapping him in his grief. He couldn't breathe nor could he wipe away the tears. He'd let them flow because each drop was a testament of the loyalty, the love, and the brother he'd los…

He could now hear the wailing sirens which were at a distance but close enough to remind him of what was at stake.

Whiteboy was dead, but that wouldn't stop the police from pursuing the description of the rental nor would it remove his face from the news. He loved Whiteboy, but right now wasn't the time to be lost in grief. There'd be a day for that.

Wiping his face with his forearm, Ace scanned the street. He needed to ditch the car and stash the choppa – fast. That would buy him time to find another set of wheels and make it back to Ariel.

Slipping the officer's gun into his pocket, he slid out of the car. The streetlights cast fractured beams across the road, creating a mix of light and shadow. He stuck to the darkness, his movements precise. Each step felt heavier than the last, but his mind had to stay sharp. He had no room for slipping.

Ten minutes would pass before Ace spotted the glowing red and white sign of a QuikTrip gas station. Beneath its radiant lights were a handful of cars parked next to pumps. His eyes locked on the closest one. It was a mid-sized sedan with a middle-aged man casually filling the tank.

Ace's focus narrowed as he approached, his steps deliberate. He glanced around the lot every few paces, taking in the gas station's layout and its occupants. Through the large storefront windows, he saw a clerk behind the counter ringing up customers.

As he turned away from his target, something else caught his eye. There was a parked car near the store's entrance. The soft fumes of exhaust were curling from its tailpipe, which said that it was still running. His pulse quickened. The car was unoccupied.

Ace swept his gaze across the lot one more time. His scrutiny was sharp and calculating. His eyes shifted back to the sedan by the pumps. He began to weigh the odds. Whatever he was going to do, he needed to do it quickly because hesitation wasn't an option.

In seven large, quick steps, Ace was up on the driver's side door of the vacant vehicle. His hand hovered over the handle as he glanced around one more time. Within an instant, he was inside and shifting the gear. Speedily, Ace whipped the car out of the parking lot and headed back for the hotel room they were staying in.

After dodging most of the main streets and weaving through a few back roads, Ace finally pulled into the parking lot of Quality Inn. The morning rays had just began creeping their way over the horizon, casting a dim glow across the lot as he eased into a parking space.

Killing the engine, he swept his eyes over the area, scanning for anything off. Nothing seemed out of the ordinary. Hell, he didn't even know what the *ordinary* was anymore.

With a slow exhale, he gripped the door handle, stepping out. Ace kept his stride steady as he crossed the dimly lit walkway. The quiet hum of the early morning filled the air as he climbed the stairwell with all his senses on high alert.

Reaching the hotel room, he took one final glance around before knocking lightly.

Click.

Upon impact, the door slightly creaked open on its own. Ace froze.

His instincts flared instantly, every nerve in his body went on *super alert*. Something wasn't right.

Immediately, Ace pulled the gun from his pocket, leveling it with his chest as he eased the door open farther.

The fuck?

His eyes darted across the room, taking in the destruction – overturned furniture, shattered lampshades, bedspreads tossed in every direction.

But no Ariel. *And no blood.*

His throat tightened. His grip on the gun clenched. His mind raced, trying to piece together possibilities. He could only imagine what the fuck happened and why.

Stepping fully into the room, Ace shut the door behind him. His grip tightened a little more, fingers twitching with restrained fury.

First Whiteboy now Ariel?

A heavy breath pushed through his nostrils, his chest boiling with rage. The room was still, but inside, a storm brewed, threatening to consume him.

He was ready to lose it, no matter the cost. But he couldn't. Not yet.

The absence of blood meant there was still a chance –a sliver of hope – that she had escaped whatever had happened here.

Before last night, he and Ariel had already mapped out contingency plans, a blueprint for survival in case they got separated. He had to stay levelheaded until he knew for sure.

Stepping over the wreckage, Ace checked the bathroom – *empty*. His pulse quickened as he moved for the room's phone. Snatching up the receiver, he dialed Ariel's number. No answer.

His jaw clenched as he pressed redial for the third time. Deep down, he already knew it was pointless. Ace had known Ariel for years, and he couldn't remember a time when she didn't answer her phone. It wasn't like her.

The knot in his gut tightened. His eyes swept the room again, this time slower, taking in every detail. Something wasn't adding up. And that fact alone made his trigger finger itch.

Setting the receiver down, Ace carefully stepped toward the door, his eyes scanning every inch of the room again – the dresser, the floor, the scattered mess.

The entire space was a disaster, but something felt off. Certain items he distinctly remembered weren't part of the chaotic wreckage.

Turning away from the door, he quickly moved back toward the bathroom. Something had caught his attention the first time. Though at first, he hadn't given it much thought. His mind had been too caught up in the wreckage and Ariel's absence.

But now, as it resurfaced in his memory, a small, knowing smile pulled at the corner of his lips. She had left him a sign.

A yellow and green flyer advertising Black History Month laid on the counter. Ace picked it up and flipped it between his fingers a few times before tapping it against the surface. She had intentionally placed the flyer where he could find it.

To anyone else, it was nothing besides a piece of junk. But to him, it was a message – a cryptic signal only he'd be able to decipher. And he had.

Now, he knew where she was headed. But getting to her? Another gamble entirely.

The stolen car was undoubtedly reported by now, maybe even equipped with a Lojack system. If that was the case, it wouldn't take much effort for them to pinpoint his exact location.

Whatever his next move was, it needed to be fast because time wasn't on his side.

CHAPTER TWO

Freshman Black

*"*R*ussia's President Putin says that nuclear warfare is an option in response to Ukraine's use of U.S. and British supplied long-range missiles to hit targets inside Russia..."*

"Putin ready to blow some shit up," Freshman said to himself, pushing away from the counter with the mini-TV sitting on it.

Catching up on the world's chaos had become part of Freshman's morning routine since waking up in the hospital. At first, it was nothing more than background noise – a bunch of talking heads arguing over things they barely understood. But after being forced to endure it daily, he found himself drawn in, intrigued by the constant shifts in power, the betrayals, and the wars, both political and street-level.

Grabbing a bowl, he poured some cereal, thinking about the plan on how he'd catch Lonzo in traffic. Lonzo had been holding things down for The Hand out in Jonesboro, but that was about to change.

Just as he was about to sit down, the broadcast flashed into a breaking news update.

Freshman froze, the milk carton still in his hand. The screen flashed, the red banner at the bottom immediately locking his attention.

"Last night, on Brocket Road, a Dekalb County police officer was brutally attacked by a man who police are now saying they think to be

Anthony Jackson. He's one of the men wanted for questioning in the murder of D.E.A. Special Agent Sophia Williams… Three days ago, D.E.A. Special Agent Sophia Williams was found dead in the Lenox Mall's parking garage from a single gunshot wound. A massive manhunt is underway for twenty-three-year-old Anthony Jackson and twenty-four-year-old Michael Turner, who authorities want for questioning…"

Freshman stared in disbelief at the photos flashing across the screen. It had been over a year since he'd last seen those faces. One belonged to his old nemesis, the other to his nemesis' right hand.

Ace. He was the same muthafucka responsible for the king's downfall – the same one who had nearly sent Freshman to his grave.

His jaw clenched, muscles tightening as tension flooded through his body. His mind threatened to drag him back to the past, but he stayed locked on the broadcast. He needed to hear all the reasons behind Ace's face being plastered on the screen.

Midway through the news story's details, Hot strolled into the kitchen, stretching and letting out a loud yawn.

Freshman spun around, eyes sharp with urgency. "Shh!" he snapped, cutting Hot off before he could say a word.

Irritation etched into his face as he turned back to the screen; his body remained tensed. This broadcast was very important, and he wasn't about to miss a single word.

"What?" Hot asked, raising an eyebrow. He stepped closer, eyes narrowing as he took in the screen. "The fuck?" he huffed incredulously. Ace's face was one he'd never forget.

"Exactly." Freshman kept his focus on the broadcast until it cut to a commercial. His jaw tightened as he envisioned the Feds getting to Ace before he could. That wasn't an option.

Shaking his head, he sneered at the screen. "That bitch ass nigga put these holes in me, left me for dead. Ain't no way I'ma let them get him first."

"What, Pee? You saying the nigga, Ace, is the one that hit you up?" Hot questioned, his face twisting in disbelief.

When Freshman first got out of the hospital, Hot had asked him over and over if he remembered who shot him. And every time, he swore he couldn't. But now there he was, saying the muthafuckin' Reaper himself had come for him and had failed. That was damn near impossible. If Ace wanted you dead, you didn't live to talk about it.

Freshman bobbed his head slowly, his jaw clenched tight. "Pussy nigga caught me down bad then took me somewhere and left me for dead. I thought I was just dreaming that shit when I saw his face, but the muthafucka, Swift…"

He caught himself, lips pressing into a thin line. He was about to say too much. The last thing he needed was Hot asking the wrong questions.

"Who?" Hot asked curiously.

"Nobody, man. Aye, so Live pulled up bout the nigga, Lonzo, talking bout he on deck and that he wanna meet cause he feel like us…"

"*Feel like us?* Man, please," Hot said, moving for the refrigerator.

"That's what I'm saying, but the nigga, Live, certain that he on the same page, so I guess we see if the nigga for real. If not, then you already know how we gon' handle it," Freshman told him after finally pouring milk into the bowl of cereal.

"Shid, we better off just handling it. Ion know why you think you can trust this nigga, Live. Nigga might be playing for the set up," Hot returned, grabbing a cup.

"Maybe, but I don't think homie on no shit like that for real. I think he knows better."

"Shawty, you killed his partna then left him with his life on the line. What the hell do he pose to be on? *I think* that shot to ya head knocked a lil sense outta you, bra," Hot said with an arched eyebrow.

"Man, shut the fuck up," Freshman snapped, instantly becoming angered. His stomach turned at the thought of the gash of his scalp which was an agonizing reminder of how close he'd come to death. His body shook from the burning urge for revenge. He hadn't thought about it since he'd left the hospital, but now, Ace's image loomed in his mind like a haunting nightmare that wouldn't easily fade away unless he faced – and ended – it.

"*Man, shut the fuck up*," Hot mocked as he poured himself a cup of apple juice. "For real tho, you be reaching for shit that just ain't there.

We can't trust these niggas, so let's just stick to what's working, which is us taking back what's ours – like you said."

"You couldn't of heard me right because *I* said I wanted *everything*. Not just some blow and money but the soldiers too. What's the point in having a kingdom with no knights?"

Hot smacked his teeth irritably. "Here you go with this shit again. Bra, there is no kingdom, only a group of niggas trying to eat. And right now, all them niggas most likely are looking at us as the niggas who trying to stop that. Pee, you…" Hot cut his words short.

He could see that Freshman was stuck on the fairytale shit and trying to change his perspective on it was pointless. "You know what? We'll handle it your way, and if it don't pan out the way you want it, just say I was right, then we gonna do it my way, ight?"

Freshman stared at him a moment before agreeing. "Bet, and now that I done seen this nigga face on the TV, I'm adding him to the agenda. I wanna kill this nigga and his lil clique."

"Pee, you didn't hear what the news said? Ace is the most wanted nigga in America right now. You think shawty gone stick around? He'd be dumb as fuck to stay in the city, especially after that lil broadcast. We need to focus on the task at hand, which is Tip. All that other shit can wait. You trying to pile too much on the plate when we haven't even tasted the food yet." Hot more than understood his reason for wanting to end Ace.

Hell, if a nigga had tried to kill him, he'd want to do the same. But trying to catch a nigga already on the run would be doing too much.

"If Ace is gone, I'll settle for his team," Freshman said, his voice laced with cold determination. His phone vibrated in his hand, an incoming call flashing across the screen. Checking the number, he stood up. "And Tip? He's already handled. Y'all just don't know it yet."

Without another word, he answered the call. "Yo…" He disappeared into the bathroom, shutting the door behind him.

Hot's eyes narrowed, suspicion creeping in as he took another sip from his cup. *This is new.* Freshman had never been the type to keep secrets – especially not from him.

Setting his cup down, Hot's gaze lingered on the closed door a little longer. He wanted to brush it off, but something felt off. Everyone had their moments of privacy, sure, but this wasn't like Freshman.

His homeboy had always been an open book, except when outsiders were around. But that was then. This was now. Something had definitely changed.

"Damn, how shit change," Hot mumbled to himself, letting his curiosity get the best of him. Stealthily, he quickly tiptoed his way over the small distance and placed his ear to the door.

"Man. I been trying to finish this shit, but it's taking longer than I thought… The fuck you mean, assistance?"

Hot's brow arched. *Why would someone be offering Freshman assistance and assistance for what?*

"Listen, I got this, aight? You just need to worry about your end of things. I heard about that lil' unfortunate situation between you and my new friends…" Freshman smirked, waiting for the threats he knew were coming. The confirmation would be subtle – a shift in tone, a hesitation, the threat – and all of it would validate what he already suspected.

Since their first encounter, Swift had controlled the board, keeping Freshman boxed into his game. He had to admit, for a while, he'd felt trapped, suffocated by Swift's grip. But then, a critical piece of intel had landed in his lap, one that changed everything.

What a fucking revelation it was. In an instant, the power dynamic shifted. Some of those cards had fallen into Freshman's hands, balancing the scales just enough to give him leverage. He now held insight into Swift's motives – this knowledge could tilt the game in his favor.

If Swift thought he'd stay a step ahead, he had another thing coming.

"Aight, we'll talk. When and where?" Freshman's eyes darted toward the door. The floor creaked on the other side. His muscles tensed, but he kept his voice even as he memorized the time and location. Once the details were set, he disconnected the call.

Staring at the darkened screen of his phone, he saw the faint reflection of his face staring back at him. A grin crept across his lips. He could almost feel the weight of the crown pressing down on his head – the power, the respect – it was finally within reach.

But this was just another step. The streets wouldn't hand him the throne without a fight. Blood would spill before it was all said and done.

Sliding the phone into his pocket, Freshman turned toward the door. He reached but didn't grab the knob. Instead, he slowly pressed his ear against the door and listened. Nothing besides the small television could be heard.

A moment passed; the floor didn't creak again. He smirked, looking at himself in the mirror.

CHAPTER THREE

Ace

"Not H.E.R… Anyway, speaking of Netflix, they are dropping a new series this week call *Blessed*. They say it's something about an old lady serial killer who thinks that her neighbors, Mary and Joseph, are about to have baby Jesus. You know I'm already hooked from the description alone," the V103 radio host said.

"See, that's how they get you. Get you all hyped up about it then have you waiting all year just to watch it. But hold on, Nina, before we go down the Netflix rabbit hole, let's take a quick news break…"

"This is your local news update provided by V103. Authorities are still searching for two suspects wanted in connection with the murder…"

Irritated, Ace reached to cut the radio off. He was beyond tired of hearing his and Whiteboy's government names being splashed all over the airwaves.

Obviously, they hadn't realized that the person wheeled out of the hotel room on the gurney was one of the men they were hunting. For now, their confusion was buying him a little more time. He knew that sooner or later, all of their efforts would be directed toward him alone.

Ace's jaw clenched as the vivid recollection of the scene flashed through his mind. Dragging knuckles across his forehead, he wanted to push past the frustration and grief. Some muthafuckas had run down on his best friend, snatching his life away. Revenge burned its way into his chest. Who was responsible? He badly wanted to…

Ace shook his head. Now wasn't the time to get emotionally lost in his thoughts. He was still a fugitive and planned on keeping it that way. After checking the time on the radio's display, Ace glanced around the street.

A few houses up from where he parked, a man was loading boxes into the back of his SUV. Across the way, a lady was putting her energetic kids into a mini van. At the house over from her, a man was pushing a lawnmower across his yard. He would be the only threat Ace needed to maneuver past to reach the destination at the far end of the street.

He remembered from the last time he'd visited that this wasn't a neighborhood where someone could just stroll around without drawing the unwanted attention of a nosy neighbor. The residents of this area were most likely the older part of the middle class – people who prided themselves on feeling safe and protected in their little corner of life. And people who wouldn't hesitate in calling law enforcement to keep it that way.

Ace glanced down at his clothes. Nothing about his outfit screamed *jogger*, so that cover story was out. Five minutes passed before his eyes saw something on the car's floorboard – a potential solution to his problem.

After relocating the vehicle a block away, he wiped down everything he'd touched and grabbed the dog leash. Now, he was just a desperate man searching for his missing dog. He moved cautiously, calling out a made-up name, whistling here and there. It didn't take long to flag down the attention of the man mowing the lawn.

The older Caucasian man shut off the mower and squinted. "Whaddya want?" he asked in a thick southern drawl.

"Hey, you seen a brown dog running around here? Pitbull, black collar." Ace held up the leash, making his lie more believable.

"A dog?" Taking the handkerchief from his pocket, he wiped his face and frowned. "Nah, I haven't seen no dog. You youngins need to learn to keep your eyes on your dogs, ya know? They'll get in all types of trouble, costing you money." The old man swept his eyes over the length of the street before looking back at him.

Ace offered a slight smile. "Yeah, you're right. I'll check on up the street. Thanks anyway." Throwing up a hand, the man returned to his mower, muttering something about loose dogs. Ace continued on toward his destination, his pulse steadying. The excuse had worked for now, but he couldn't shake the feeling that the man's eyes were still on him.

Ace stole another glance over his shoulder as he continued calling out his imaginary dog's name. He had finally reached the driveway of the house he and Ariel had marked as their last-minute refuge.

The couple who owned the place were loyal customers of hers – and according to Ariel, they'd jump at any chance to climb higher on her *owed favors* list. Ace didn't know them personally, but if Ariel trusted them –and this house – enough to bet their safety on it, who was he to argue?

He whistled and called out the name one last time. The mowing man had finally turned his back, pushing the machine toward the far side of the yard.

Seizing the moment, Ace crouched low, moving swiftly along the side of the house, his body hugging the wall. His ears tuned in to every sound – the distant hum of the mower, the faint crunch of dried leaves beneath his feet, the measured rhythm of his own breath.

At the back of the house, he spotted the door. But something else caught his attention. A small fence was the only thing separating this property from the one behind it. The sight made him freeze. The house beyond was in plain view. If he could see into its windows, that meant someone inside could see him just as easily.

His retinas narrowed as his gaze darted between windows, scanning for any sign of life. Nothing. Taking a slow breath, Ace tested the door. The knob turned. Without hesitation, he slipped inside.

Ace shut the door swiftly, sealing out the world behind him. His gaze swept over the darkened room where slivers of light seeped through the blinds, casting jagged shadows along the walls. He paused, allowing his eyes to adjust. His breath slowed, and his heartbeat became steady as he listened for any sign that he wasn't alone.

Then – a creak.

His grip tightened around the pistol, the muscles in his neck and chest coiled, until a familiar silhouette emerged from the darkness. Ariel.

"Ace?" Her voice quivered with emotion.

Before he could answer, she closed the space between them, throwing her arms around his neck. He held her tightly, feeling the tremor of relief coursing through her body as she pressed against his. For the first time in what felt like forever, the weight in Ace's chest lightened.

Ariel pulled back just enough to meet his gaze, searching his eyes.

"I thought I lost you," she said as a tear glistened its way down the side of her face.

Ace smiled. "You ain't gonna lose me, A." He leaned in, pressing his lips against hers. The warmth of the moment was brief – too brief. Pulling back, his expression turned serious. "What happened at the hotel?"

Ariel exhaled, shaking her head. "Bae, I don't know honestly. I was trying to call you when somebody started knocking on the door, saying he was hotel staff checking on residents. But when I looked through the peephole, he didn't look like nobody who worked there. So, I grabbed the gun and called the front desk. Just like I thought, they said he didn't. Security came up, but by the time they got to my door, he was gone."

She hesitated, her brows drawing together. "But the way he talked, it was weird. He had this thick accent… like one of them Italian muthafuckas straight out of a mafia movie."

"Italian?" Instinctively, Ace's jaw tightened. Had Paul sent his little minions to follow them? More than likely. Paul had already proven he liked to know everything, yet Ace had been foolish enough to underestimate just how far he'd go.

"Yeah… Italian." Ariel's expression shifted as the weight of the situation settled in. The pounding at the hotel door had felt off, but when she connected it to the people Ace was dealing with, she knew things were more than serious.

Ace shook his head, his anger rising as the pieces clicked into place. When him and Whiteboy had gone to see Paul, the vibe had been unmistakable. Paul had lured them to that warehouse to tie off a loose end. But Ace's quick thinking had brought them time. The only thing keeping him alive was the information he held.

Whiteboy though? He wasn't as valuable.

If those mafia motherfuckers had been tailing them, they would have misread him and Whiteboy splitting up and probably took it as a move against Paul's wishes. Ace now saw the truth. Whiteboy getting gunned down wasn't some random act.

They wouldn't be stupid enough to kill Ace. But Whiteboy? He was expendable. A sacrificial lamb. His death was a warning.

Only Paul had made a fatal mistake. He'd fucked with a man who had nothing left to lose and everything to destroy.

Ace exhaled slowly, fingers locking behind his head as his mind raced through every move that led to this. No second guessing. No turning back.

"Fuck! Them motherfuckers ran down on Whitebo…"

"We need to leave, Ace…" Ariel blurted, cutting him off. She could already see the storm brewing in his mind. He was on the run, Whiteboy was dead, and with the life growing inside of her, she couldn't afford to get caught in the crossfire.

Ace's eyes narrowed. "Yeah, I can – after I get those diamonds and pay them back for White. A, you know I can't run without real paper."

"I know, bae, but we can go to Queen's. She's got a whole network for shit like this. I know she'll…"

"A!" His voice cut through her words, sharp with aggression. "I'm not leaving 'til I do all these motherfuckers in and get them stones. Everything we built was destroyed by them and Kero. I walked away once. Not this time. I'm finishing this shit."

Ariel stared at him for a long moment. She understood – more than she wanted to – but accepting it was another thing entirely. A life was growing inside her, a life that needed him. But how could he be there with everything working against him?

She was torn between what she wanted and the cold reality in front of her. Ace was fighting against all odds, standing on the edge with no easy way back up. And if she truly wanted to see him through this, she couldn't afford to be at odds with him. He needed her support – completely. That meant securing herself, so his focus could stay on surviving.

"You're right…" she uttered, her voice softer now. "I need you to handle it. Ace, we have a future to think about."

She reached for his hand, gently placing it over her stomach.

Ace's hand flinched, almost going limp. His gaze locked onto hers, the weight of realization crashing down on him. The very thing he had spent years trying to avoid was now his reality – and the worst part? He couldn't recall a single moment when he'd actually tried to prevent it.

Ever since Ariel had come into his life, he had let himself slip, indulging in the moment without a second thought. Not once had he stopped to consider the consequences. Not once had he imagined that this could be the outcome. Now, here it was, staring him in the face.

Regret clawed at his chest, raw and unrelenting. He wasn't just thinking about this child; he was thinking about the one before, the one he never gave a chance. The past had already branded him a destroyer, and now, once again, his reckless choices could possibly lead another innocent life into the crossfire. How desperate – and how careless – had he been — and would be?

The truth stung like an open wound. He was still the same ol' Ace, dragging people into his chaos, forcing them to bear the weight of his selfish urges. And now, for the first time, he had to ask himself: *What the fuck am I supposed to do about it?*

Ariel stepped closer, her hand cupping the side of Ace's stunned face. "I get it," she murmured, her voice steady. "But this life? This life was created by circumstances – and love. And that's exactly why you're gonna do what has to be done. You've fought too hard to let them take what's yours – what's ours." Her tone sharpened, eyes blazing with resolve. "So, do what the fuck you gotta do, Ace. Be the last man standing because there's a future waiting for us, and *you* will be in it."

She leaned in, her lips brushing against his, a silent promise sealed in the moment. Ariel knew he needed time to process it all, and she hated that he had to find out like this – with the world already closing in on him. But keeping it from him would've been worse.

Ariel inhaled deeply, pushing away her own doubts. She was having this baby. And Ace? He was going to be in its life. No matter what.

Ace stepped back, finding a chair and sinking into it. He dragged a hand over his face, exhaling sharply. Ariel moved, settling onto his thigh, her fingers running across his scalp. Their eyes locked.

"I gotta get you that money, so you can make it home and get you a place," Ace said. "Then, I'ma find Paul and kill him. After that, we leave for good, A."

"I'm with you," Ariel said, tilting his chin up, forcing him to meet her gaze. "But promise me something."

"I'm listening."

"If shit gets too heavy, you call me. Let me help. This is big, Ace. I can't afford for you to be stubborn. You're one man against too damn many."

Ace nodded slowly. "Aight. But I won't be alone. I think I know somebody who might be willing to help." He paused. "How much cash you got on hand?"

"I think it's a thousand or two," Ariel said. "But I won't need much to get up there, so you can take most of it. Bae, we need to figure out how you're gonna move around. You're America's most wanted."

"I got something in mind."

"Like what?" she asked, stroking the side of his head.

"Like the muthafuckas who move around every day without anyone paying them any attention."

Ariel's brow arched. Plenty of people moved around unnoticed – until they gave a reason to be. She needed him to be more specific. "Like who?"

"Like a stankin ass homeless person, wandering, looking for a place to be," Ace said. "Think about it – bums and junkies roam the whole city, and nobody questions them unless they're somewhere they're not supposed to be."

A smirk appeared on Ariel's face. She'd considered a few disguises he might pass with, but his idea far – likely – exceeded hers. The thought of Ace as a homeless man was almost funny, but damn, it was brilliant.

"I'm hitting the thrift store to grab you some things. You need to make a quick list of everything you'll need right now."

"I really don't need shit but some thrift clothes and a roll-up coat or something. Matter fact, maybe some zip ties. I'm paying Kero's sister a visit first. I know he stashed some paper with her, so she's getting it. Then, I gotta find Trigga. Bra the only one I can think of that a help me with those mafia muthafuckas.

"A, you leaving by tomorrow, ight? And while you're out, grab two burner phones and activate them, so we can stay in contact." Ace stood, scratching the palm of his hand. "Matter fact, let me put some thought into this list."

CHAPTER FOUR

Louis Gram

"The motherfucker slides the window up then sticks the upper half of his body through. Now, it's only his legs and ass left, and I mean they are just there. I'm yelling, 'Get the fuck down! Get down!'"

Heading toward the break room, Gram could hear Bob Kohler's loud mouth echoing from down the corridor. A thick gutted patrol officer with a buzz cut and a gift for talking a person's head off, Kohler had a reputation for being a walking PA system – noisy, opinionated, and never out of stories. Most of them exaggerated. All of them irritating. That was how Gram came to know the man without a formal introduction.

The Zone Six precinct had the feel of a small fraternity house – two floors and a basement split between an operations center and a low-level break area. The whole place looked more like a repurposed community center than a law enforcement hub. Gram figured whoever came up with the design had never seen a real precinct before.

Within the first week, Gram realized that the small place was no match for the obnoxious *Bob Kohler* rants. Gram had managed to avoid speaking to the guy. So far, it was a personal victory.

Gram walked in. The space reeked of burnt coffee, the usual scent of exhaustion, bad takeout, and over-exaggerated banter. Kohler sat at the table with another uniformed officer. Detective Mike Garner –a broad-shouldered, arrogant individual known for his dry humor – leaned against the counter with his arms crossed.

Gram ignored all three of the men, heading straight for the coffee pot. He wasn't here to make acquaintances.

"Well, well," Kohler's voice boomed, cutting through the room. "You're the new guy, huh? The one everybody's trying to figure out?"

Gram didn't respond, pouring his coffee. He wondered where small packets of Sweet'N Low were.

"Now don't be shy. We're all on the same team, with the same job, *right*?" Kohler chuckled. "Where you from? They say you talk like a DC guy. DC guys are all stuck-up."

Gram exhaled sharply through his nose, stirring in a sugar packet. He wasn't in the mood for this.

Kohler wasn't done. "Shit, you don't say much either, do you?"

Again, Gram didn't respond.

"You don't talk, and nobody knows you. Are you military?"

Gram's grip tightened on the coffee cup. He turned slightly, making eye contact with Garner, who smirked like he was enjoying the show.

"Let me guess. That's supposed to be classified too?" Kohler laughed, nudging his buddy. "See, around here, we're a tightknit fami-ly." He gestured before interlocking his fingers. "Everyone knows everyone's history, backgrounds. This is what makes us *fit* together, you could say. It helps at building some level of trust. Can you imagine going into combat with someone you don't know?"

Gram turned back to his coffee, jaw clenched. He had three options: engage, ignore, and *ignore* again. Though he decided on the fourth – be cordial, be brief and straightforward, then smile and finish the damn coffee to get what he needed before he left.

"Where are my manners?" Gram set the coffee on the counter and crossed his hands in front of him. "I'm Detective Gram. I was born. I grew up. I went to school, then I went to college. I graduated; I worked a job. Now I'm here with you – him and him," Gram finished, nodding his head at the other two present. He wanted to pat himself on the back for the briefest history ever given orally.

Kohler smiled, even though he didn't seem too happy about the response. "Damn, that was informative." He slowly clapped his hands. "Real American dream shit. You should write a book.

"Hey, Garner…" Kohler called out, turning his attention to him. "We finally did it. We finally got ourselves a real *asshole* in the building."

Gram smirked, giving no reaction besides taking a sip from his coffee. He had always been an *asshole*.

Kohler leaned forward onto his elbows, placing his eyes back on Gram. The uniform tightened around his biceps, causing his arms to seem bigger than they were. "And luckily for you, Detective Gram, I just so happen to be an *asshologist*." He brought his hand up, like he was about to let him in on a secret. "That means I'm an expert when it comes to assholes and *assholing*."

The three snickered like a trio of little girls. Gram was impressed. Bob Kohler had held his attention close to a minute now. "That would explain the smell."

Someone coughed a chuckle down. Kohler's face tightened. He forced his lips into a grin. "I'd rather smell like shit than be a federal police-rat any day. You fucking Feds love to sneak your asses down here, sniffing around, trying to find anything on the good men and women who put their lives on the line every day protecting the country's streets. I don't like them, I don't like you, and I especially don't like smug son of bitches who think they're smarter than everybody else."

Gram sighed, bored of being a *smug* son of a bitch. And he was tired of Kohler's childish rancor. The boy needed to be put back in a child's place. He met Kohler's stare unblinkingly.

"Did that make you feel any better?" Gram asked with a raised eyebrow. "Did them *tough* words make you feel manly, *Officer*? I hope they made your day, and for the record, no, I'm not a Fed. I'm a detective who does not think that he's smarter than everybody else. No." Gram shook his head to add emphasis. "No, it's quite the contrary. I actually think that most people are smarter than me, especially you, Mr. Kohler. And right now, it's been proven." Gram's tone lowered a bit. Kohler's expression said that he was curious as to where Gram was taking this.

"At this very moment," Gram continued, "you are the smartest person in this room because your ass didn't leave that seat to put some pressure behind them meaningless words."

Kohler abruptly jumped to his feet from the chair – his posture a little *too* aggressive, his stare piercing.

Gram was partly amused. Just as quick as he'd given the man a compliment about being smart, he was about to prove that he wasn't. "Come a little closer now."

No more than ten feet of space laid between the two egos. Gram quickly realized by the petty officer's stance that he was not ready for what he was about to issue. There were three different forms of martial arts in his self-defense arsenal that he could exercise in a split second. However, he'd let Kohler's next move pick.

Kohler's foot lifted before they all heard the heavy voice come from the hallway. Everyone's eyes went to the door.

"Is there a problem?" the precinct commander, James Bois, questioned upon entering the room. The commander was a short, dark-skinned man who favored Kid's father in the movie, *House Party*. His attitude was stern. He didn't change or bend for anyone. Recently, Gram learned that the man's strict demeanor was the same regardless of the time of day.

All eyes were on the commander. "Good," the commander finally uttered, letting his retinas linger on Kohler longer than the others. Then, he locked on to Gram. "My office..." he told him, sweeping over everyone else again and leaving.

Kohler took his seat as Gram moved for the door. "Gram, me and you gonna get to know each other real good before it's all said and done." He grinned.

"That will be your mistake," Gram returned over his shoulder. It was nine-thirty in the morning, and Commander Bois had personally summoned him for a chat.

Gram quickly figured that this was probably about to be one of those *talks* Bois was known for giving when he wanted you to help his narrow mind understand why you – in so many words – had failed to do some*thing* according to his standards.

Within the few weeks Gram had been here, he'd encountered four of these where he politely and respectfully let him know – in so many words – that his way of doing things wouldn't conflict with the interest of the commander. Therefore, he'd acknowledge the commander's policy, but he would not change or conform to his way of getting things done. The commander was having a hard time gradually accepting it.

Stepping into the biggest office within the precinct, Gram eased the door closed. Commander Bois sat behind his desk where he began scribbling on paperwork with a rhythm that suggested this conversation was more than a formality. He didn't look up from the papers when he told Gram, "You're being reassigned."

Gram's brows furrowed. "Reassigned?"

Bois gave a nod before setting his eyes on him. There was nothing in his expression to be read. It was just a plain fact dropped on the table like a big bombshell.

"Hold on, Commander Bois. I finally got a solid lead on the Corey West and Kesha Mills case," Gram protested. He stepped forward as if closing the distance would sway the man's decision. "Give me at least two more weeks, and I'll have it solved, then *you* can send me wherever you like."

The moment Gram stepped foot inside the Zone Six precinct, the air shifted. It wasn't hostile, but it sure as hell wasn't *welcoming* either. He immediately felt like an intruder – an outsider in a tightly wound circle that had no interest in expanding. The brief glances, the murmured conversations that halted as he passed, the way officers either stared too long or refused to meet his eyes, all told him the same thing. This wasn't an invitation into some brotherhood. It was a silent warning.

He got the message loud and clear. But what could he do? His mission came first, and now, a reassignment was threatening to snatch it from his grasp. The weight of it pressed on his mental. He wasn't here to make friends, but he'd be damned if they were going to make it hard to do his job.

"Gram, it ain't my call. The *chief* wants you downtown immediately. Maybe you can tell me what's this about because she damn sure did not." The commander stared at him curiously. Commander Bois was expecting an answer.

The chief? Gram's mind kicked into overdrive. His file had a list of supposed specialties, but none of them were extraordinary enough to warrant personal interest from a police chief. He was a solid detective, one who prided himself on his record, but nothing about him screamed special assignment material. He'd reviewed the file more than once, making sure the details aligned with his own reality. And yet, here he was, being shuffled around like a pawn on a board he hadn't even seen.

Plus, reassignments didn't happen this fast — not unless you'd proven yourself or someone had other plans for you. Standards were met before opportunities were granted. That was the unspoken rule across all law enforcement departments. But this? This was different. Someone had pulled a string.

Gram exhaled slowly, his fingers tapping against his thigh. This wasn't just a bureaucratic decision. Someone high up wanted him somewhere else. *But why? And more importantly, who?*

His jaw mildly twitched. This didn't have the feel of being random; it felt very directed. And there was only one person he could think of as the *director* of such a move. *But again why?*

"Maybe the *chief* can tell you — and me — why." Gram turned, leaving the commander frowning in thought.

Back in the homicide unit, Gram barely acknowledged the two detectives who hadn't even glanced his way upon his entrance. He was used to being invisible here. They all acted as if he — and his tiny excuse for a workspace — didn't exist. That was fine by him. The less attention, the better.

With purpose, he made his way to his so-called workstation — a glorified storage closet of an office. A battered backroom desk, a handful of scattered documents, and a Dollar General trash can set in the corner, completing the picture of utter insignificance. The rolling chair looked like it had been snatched from a thrift store's clearance section, and the Sunday school bulletin board on the wall? That was the real kicker. It was like they'd thrown in a little decoration to make it seem like he belonged, as if he was actually part of the *guys*.

Gram smirked at the thought, shaking his head. If this was their idea of a warm welcome, he'd hate to see what their outright hostility looked like.

He grabbed his duffle bag and began pulling out the few things he owned. A few weeks of investigating hadn't given him enough time to turn this closet-sized hole into a real analyzing zone of criminality. Not that it would've made a difference. The environment itself wasn't built for him. It was built to remind him he didn't belong.

One thumbtack at a time, he took down each photograph from the board, each image that of a story cut short too soon. When he reached the last one, Gram hesitated.

Kesha Mills.

She stood frozen in time, her dark skin glowing with the promise of a future she'd never get to live. Her smile radiated the kind of joy only a young girl with dreams could have – the kind of joy that no one had the right to steal.

Gram's fingers tightened around the edges of the photo. He felt that familiar fire smoldering in his chest, the same one that always ignited when he looked into the face of a Black child whose soul was still waiting on justice.

"I promise you, Kesha Mills," he murmured, voice low but firm, "I'm going to bring you justice before I'm done with Atlanta."

Lying the picture atop the thin pile of pictures and case notes, he exhaled, glancing around the room. Same shit, different day.

Detective McCormick sat hunched over his laptop, sipping his morning brew like it held the secrets of the universe. A few desks over, Detective Bradford mumbled into his phone, flipping through a file as if the words on the pages bored him.

Gram moved with purpose, swiftly sliding the folder into his briefcase.

By protocol, all case files were to be turned over to his immediate supervisor – the commander.

But Gram already knew what would happen if he followed the rules. The file would sit on the commander's desk, untouched, until it was buried beneath a pile of reports deemed more *urgent*. When the secretary eventually cleaned up, she'd toss it onto some detective's desk like an afterthought. The lucky detective – whoever it was –

would skim it, shrug, and shove it into a cabinet labeled OGI – *On-Going Investigation,* a nice way of saying *never solved.* That wouldn't be the case this time.

Gram had seen it happen too many times to count, the slow, silent burial of a case file. He often wondered if a real internal investigation ever looked into how cases were handled, who'd be the first to get fired. He might just get his answer if Commander Bois refused to let him finish what he started.

Adjusting the duffle's strap on his shoulder, Gram grabbed his briefcase and quietly walked out.

Something big was happening, and he intended to find out what.

The ride to Atlanta's police headquarters was short – too short. It barely gave Gram enough time to make two important calls. First on his list was the light of his life, his sixteen-year-old daughter, Emmy. She was the busiest teenager he knew, always caught up in something, whether it was school, social causes, or whatever latest trend had her attention.

Whenever he found a free moment when working a case, he made it a point to call her. Lately though, those calls were feeling more like check-ins than real conversations. His little munchkin, once so eager to chat his ear off, now gave him quick updates: the last thing she ate, a message from her mother, a rushed "I love you, Daddy" before she had to go.

Gram hated it. If he could stop time, he would. He didn't want her growing up too fast. He didn't want her exposed to the world and all its harsh realities. For forty-two years, he had seen and experienced enough darkness to make him fear for her future. The world wasn't getting any better. It was unraveling, becoming a place unfit for the innocent. Yet, here he was, doing everything in his power to make it safer, not just for her but for every child like her.

And that, more than anything, fueled his determination.

He couldn't just lock her away in a protective bubble. His eyes couldn't hover over her every step, ensuring she always walked the safest path. He wasn't omnipresent and never would be. The thought frustrated him, but he knew better than to let it get to him.

His own father had been overbearing, obsessed with control, and that obsession had driven Gram's only sister to despise him. That was a lesson Gram refused to ignore. He would never imitate his father's mistakes. Instead, he made sure his presence alone was enough to keep Emmy safe.

Back home in Perry, Florida, she lived with his ex-wife in the same town where his name carried weight. From his days as a junior light-weight boxer to his reputation as a highly decorated soldier, he had built a legacy that spoke volumes. People still murmured about 'Fuck 'Em Up Gram', the man who loved his family more than anything. In that small corner of the country, no one was reckless enough to test his limits.

After that call, Gram fetched the black phone The Figure had given him. Its purpose was to be the main line of their communication. But as he dialed for the fourth time with no response, he wasn't surprised. The Figure, much like his daughter, was always moving, always busy. The difference was, once he saw those missed calls, he would answer. And Gram knew, when that response finally came, it would mean something.

Taking a deep breath, Gram's mind started to wander. He hated walking into situations blindly and unprepared. But as much as he hated uncertainty, he doubted the Atlanta Police Department would have him drive downtown only to inform him that his cover had been blown. If he were really under suspicion of impersonating an officer, there would be no need for a polite summons to headquarters; his arrest would've already been attempted back at Zone Six.

The news of his alleged transgression would have traveled fast, like a wildfire through the small fortress of the precinct. He could practically see Bob Kohler's *smug* smile approaching as he'd be forced to face the inevitable. "War Zone" – that was how they'd describe the chaos that would ensue.

As he approached the four-story building, Gram took a long, steadying breath, gathering himself for whatever was to come. Inside, he was led to the uncomfortable waiting area. He sat for almost twenty minutes before he was finally escorted to the office of Chief Jennifer Wilkins.

The elevator ride was brief, and Gram couldn't help but notice the young woman accompanying him. She was one of those people who seemed to know everyone and everything, greeting people in the halls, laughing with this person, pointing out some unknown gossip to that one. She made the trip to the third floor seem like a parade as they passed by desks and cubicles. She stopped in front of a door, its bold black lettering reading Chief Jennifer Wilkins.

His gut tightened. Something about this felt wrong. But he couldn't turn back now. Gram had read the chief's dossier prior to coming to Atlanta. Learning exactly whose turf you were lying a foot on was always first in any operation.

Jennifer Wilkins graduated top of her class and with high honors from the Georgia Police Academy, earning her a reputation for intelligence and tactical proficiency. Leadership skills went without saying.

After making a name for herself in the department, Ms. Wilkins transitioned to SWAT where she became the first young, Black female officer to join the unit. She quickly excelled and moved on to detective work, beginning to carve out her mark on the city of Atlanta. Impressively, she maintained an astonishing ninety-two percent case closure rate, earning her the title of the youngest – and most efficient – detective in APD history. But that was just the beginning.

By the age of twenty-five, thanks to her impeccable track record, she was handpicked to take on a leading role in hunting down one of the country's most brutal serial killers, The Heckler.

Gram had heard the grim stories of the ex-Green Beret turned psychopath. At the time, Gram was running a covert operation overseas, but that didn't stop him from hearing about the six-foot-three, long-haired man with steel-grey eyes who'd gruesomely murdered eight senators and eleven lobbyists along with fourteen civilians. For many, it was a tragic loss, but for others, it was a dark blessing.

Then, there was the pretty, brown-skinned teenage girl who America had chosen to bring this experienced war veteran to justice. At best, Gram knew it was a move to end her career – or even her life. He wasn't the only one who caught on. A day into the manhunt, outrage spread across the country from the upper and middle class, basically those who had far more reason to fear The Heckler than the poor ever would.

Never in his forty-two years had he seen such widespread anger and disdain aimed at ol' Uncle Sam for depending on a young girl, who some mockingly called the *Valedian School Girl,* to lead the cavalry. Why wasn't the government sending in their toughest Navy SEALs from its elite forces?

Headlines and mountains of articles about how foreign nations, particularly the Russians, were laughing at the U.S. quickly gained traction. It wasn't long before the media storm took off, and soon the slogan *Enough Was Enough* was splashed across news outlets everywhere.

From one coast to the other, the press heralded the supposed turning point. As the public uproar reached its peak, whispers of reprimands for the agencies who had so easily used a beautiful, innocent soul as a scapegoat filled the air. They couldn't even handle one of their own – an internal problem blown far out of proportion – and now it was coming back to haunt them.

One day, POTUS finally decided to address America – and the world – on the matter. Conclusions were stamped: the president was about to shutdown the circus and serve the public Thomas Bullock's head on a platter. Gram, and a majority of the country, was certain of this.

However, the POTUS stunned the nation with his response – not only endorsing Ms. Wilkins' role in capturing the Heckler but also openly challenging the infamous assassin to turn him into the same public spectacle as the senators before him. To the average citizen, it was a bold, defiant move, a display of unwavering confidence in American security. But to those with real field experience, it was reckless posturing.

Thomas Bullock's IQ was an astounding 185. His mind was a finely tuned instrument of warfare, his body honed by grueling training that had pushed the limits of human endurance. He was a walking arsenal, even without a single weapon in his possession. Given the right conditions, he could take over a small town – maybe even two – before encountering anyone capable of matching his skillset.

But the White House was no town. It was a fortress, safeguarded by elite operatives who had mastered the art of precision combat. If

Bullock ever made it past the gates, his lethal expertise would be met with an even deadlier force, one that would respond with cold, calculated brutality.

Long story short – as intriguing as it was – Jennifer Wilkins shocked everyone, cementing yet another milestone in her already impressive career.

Six weeks into the manhunt, the body count had risen to thirty-seven civilians, including eighteen fallen law enforcement officers. Yet, against all odds, the future police chief of Atlanta single-handedly brought the most feared man in America to his knees – without backup, without reinforcements, just sheer will and precision.

Heads spun. Eyebrows raised. Conspiracy theories spread like wildfire. How could the *Valedian School Girl*, a young, Black woman, humble the nation's most dangerous predator, a figure who had eluded the best minds and marksmen in the country? In doing so, she had unknowingly shaken the very foundation of the machismo-driven society. The rest, as they say, is history.

Gram stepped into the office of Chief Jennifer Wilkins, the youngest police chief in the south. The space was neat, every item in its rightful place, a reflection, he assumed, of the woman sitting behind the desk. One look at her told him everything he needed to know. She was sharp, disciplined, and carried herself with a quiet but unmistakable authority.

Her short, neatly styled hair framed a face that was serious yet likeable. She didn't need to raise her voice or throw around her weight to command respect. Her presence alone was enough. She reminded him of a house cat, seemingly soft, composed, even inviting. But beneath that skin laid something cunning, something lethal – a predator waiting for the right moment to pounce.

She barely looked up from the file in front of her. "Detective Louis Gram," she said, her voice measured. She finally met his eyes. "Take a seat."

Gram remained standing. "I'm good. I need to know what this is about and why I'm being reassigned?" He came – now he wanted to know.

Wilkins leaned back in her chair, fingers tapping against the armrest. "First, this is my city, so I do what the *fuck* I want, to *who* I want. Especially *those* under my watch. And reassigned?" She let out a small, humorless chuckle. "Wouldn't you agree that *redirected* would be the better word for it? But that's an *issue* I'll pass on for the time being. So, we're here now…"

The way she stared at him caused Gram to quickly rethink his approach. The Figure was a powerful man but even he'd have a hard time trying to untangle this if it just so happened to turn into a ball of chaotic interactions. She was the police chief of a major city with a *contractor* running around posing as one of her own. Placing himself on this lady's list of *things to do* wasn't an option.

Gram decided to take a seat. "So, we're here now?"

Chief Wilkins folded her hands together. "A dear friend of yours and mines *recommended* you as the man for a particular job that the city's been two days in."

Gram's eyes narrowed. "And what might that be?" *The city was two days in?* Gram adjusted his posture a little. Whatever called for the attention of the entire establishment of Atlanta was a little *too* big for his comfort and too far beyond the boundaries set by his chosen line of work. Big was bad because big always brought bad media attention.

She didn't blink. "You haven't spoken with Senator Peters?"

Gram turned the name over in his mind a few times. He didn't recall hearing it before, though the man was a senator. This alone told him all he needed to hear for the time being. Later, he'd receive a call detailing certain instructions. Gram now realized that this was somehow linked to his *overall* mission. He couldn't wait to find out how.

"Not today," Gram said, his tone unreadable. What did she have to gain by him flat out acknowledging that he hadn't known the man? If Senator Peters made it seem that way, then so be it.

An eyebrow inched upward as Chief Wilkins slid a file across the desk. Her voice was smooth yet carried a tone that suggested she wasn't in the habit of repeating herself.

"You're taking the lead position on the taskforce investigating the murder of Special Agent Sophia Williams of the DEA. At the moment, we only have two persons of interest. Names, last known residences, everything we've scraped together is in that file." She leaned back slightly, folding her arms. "Unfortunately, that's all we have so far. You'll have to put those good two legs of yours to use and obtain what the DEA has feverishly refused to hand over." Her lips curved into something that wasn't quite a smirk. "I'm sure you're familiar with the routine."

Gram didn't respond right away. His throat had gone dry but not because of nervousness. Leading a taskforce investigating the death of a DEA agent while they already had suspects identified? Something didn't sit right. If they had names and locations, why wasn't the DEA running this themselves? Why was he being pulled into what seemed like an open-and-shut case?

He wasn't about to play bounty hunter around Atlanta for free. He was good at finding people – damn good. But the last time he checked, that wasn't the job he signed up for.

The Figure had obviously forgotten the terms of their agreement. Tonight, Gram would more than remind him.

He exhaled slowly and finally spoke, his voice even but edged with skepticism.

"And the specifics of your expectations, Chief?"

Wilkins didn't miss the shift in his tone. She studied him for a beat before responding. "I expect you to do what you do best, Mr. Gram – find the truth. The DEA is keeping things close to the chest, which means this is bigger than they're letting on. That's where you come in."

Her gaze became sharp. "I don't like loose ends. And I definitely don't like being left in the dark. So, consider it your first priority to shed some light on what's really going on."

Gram glanced at the file but didn't touch it yet. He had the distinct feeling that once he did, he'd be stepping into something far more tangled than Wilkins was letting on.

Though he was already in the room. Which meant, one way or another, he was already involved.

"And the specifics of your *real assignment*," Wilkins continued, "will be given to you by Senator Peters himself."

She stood, her solid stare locking onto his. "Whatever this is, it's bigger than the usual, and if you're smart, you'll take orders without too many questions. Like me, Peters does – and gets – what he wants. He's made it very clear that you are what he wants. I bet you can imagine the Feds' reaction to this." She laughed half-heartedly. For the first time since he'd been in her presence, he caught a brief glimpse of the sweet schoolgirl the media had portrayed her as.

"Your quarters are located on the fourth floor. Once you get off the elevator, turn to your left and just walk until you see the bold black letters that read, *WPTF*. It stands for Wilkins Primary Taskforce, in case you or any of those so-called *liaison assholes* needed a reminder about who's running shit down here." She smiled. "Have a nice day, *Detective* Gram."

As soon as Chief Jennifer Wilkins dismissed Gram, the office door swung open, and a man in a black suit stepped in without saying a word. His face was blank, his posture rigid. Without any hesitation, he gestured for Gram to follow.

Gram took a second, glancing back at Wilkins, but she was already focused on something else, flipping through files on her desk like their conversation had never happened. He knew better than to ask another question regarding what she'd said, yet that hadn't been his *overall* intention.

The suited man led him through the headquarters, through the sea of officers who barely gave them a glance – this kind of thing happened all the time. They stepped through the entrance main doors where a black SUV with heavy tinted windows set at the curb. The door swung open. Gram got in.

Sitting in the backseat was who he guessed to be Senator Peters. He didn't look at Gram immediately. A text needed to be sent from his phone before. He finally raised his eyes to Gram.

"Detective Gram." His voice was smooth, like it belonged amongst the scene of a smoky jazz lounge. "We finally meet."

The suited man shut the door behind him as if the man sitting before him was someone accustomed to being in control. The atmosphere inside carried the rich scent of expensive leather, faint cigar smoke, and the deep, musky cologne of a man who knew power and *overindulgence*.

Senator Peters looked the part – salt and pepper hair slicked back, a silk pocket square neatly tucked into his tailored navy suit. If Gram had to guess, the senator had spent most of his prime in dimly lit lounges, whiskey in hand, a woman on his lap, and a band playing just the right tune for it to be a promising night for him. Even now, with years of politics shaping him, he carried that effortless cool, a relic of a life where charm and influence went hand in hand.

"I'm Senator Amor Peters. I've heard a lot about you," Peters said, studying him. "A mutual friend of *ours* – whom I don't have to name – insisted that I pull all the necessary strings to put you not only on this case but at the head of it. The murder of DEA Special Agent Sophia Williams."

Gram didn't react because he'd heard the same from Chief Wilkins. He'd let the man, on his own accord, lay out the *specifics*. Playing to Peter's fancy would hopefully reveal everything he'd use when he was reminding their *mutual friend* about the terms of *their* agreement.

Peters leaned in slightly. "This means you are to focus on Paul Manterio and his organization specifically. That's where this is going to end," he stated matter-of-factly.

Gram exhaled, already knowing where this was going. "I thought there were already two suspects of interest."

Peters smiled, but it wasn't warm. It was the kind of smile a man gave when he already knew the next ten moves. "Then work that angle all the way up to Manterio. And more importantly," he paused, tapping his fingers against the armrest, "find out who actually put those two names on the news. I want *proof* that the information is wrong."

Gram kept his expression plain, but he caught the underlying message. Peters wasn't just looking for a conviction; he wanted a narrative controlled.

"Whatever you need to get this done," Peters continued, "I'm a call away. Atlanta is my city."

Gram found it amusing that two people had said the same about Atlanta being theirs yet were using him as a tool to bring about some end in *their* city.

CHAPTER FIVE

Ace

After yanking the curtain aside, Ace peered through the window for what felt like the hundredth time. The street outside was as empty as it had been the last dozen times he checked, but it didn't ease the tightness in his chest. Letting the curtain fall back into place, he dropped onto the sofa, resting his head against the armrest. His nerves were shot.

Ariel had been gone for over two hours now, two long, agonizing hours where his mind had done nothing but churn out scenario after scenario, each one worse than the last. When he wasn't trying to rationalize her delay, he was flinching at every sudden noise, his body tensing as if expecting the walls to come crashing down around him. At this point, every sound felt like an alarm, every movement outside a potential threat.

Ace exhaled sharply, pressing his fingers against his temple. He needed to calm his mental. His thoughts were moving too fast, crashing into each other, each one taking center stage in his mind for barely a second before another shoved its way in. It was a relentless cycle, leaving him scrambling for answers that refused to come.

But the real question was whether there was even a solution. Was there really a way out of this mess, or was he just fooling himself into believing he still had control?

His jaw tightened. He hated feeling cornered, uncertain, vulnerable. He needed to do something. Anything. But first, he had to figure out if there was even a next move left to make.

The odds were stacked against him, some so insurmountable that they felt like death sentences waiting to be served. He had killed Stacey, and somehow, the Feds had gotten hold of information tying him to the murder. That part didn't sit right with him. He had been careful, meticulous. No loose ends – at least none that should have led back to him.

Yet, after learning of Kero's deceit, the puzzle pieces started falling into place. The man had already proven he couldn't be trusted, and if he had a way to benefit from Ace going down, there was no doubt in his mind that he'd take it.

Still, only two people outside his team knew about his involvement – Kero and Paul. But Paul giving him up?

That didn't make sense. Turning Ace over to the Feds wouldn't just be out of character; it would be a tactical mistake. Paul didn't seem like the type to rely on law enforcement when handling problems. If anything, he'd clean up his own mess the way men like him always did – with blood. If Paul had wanted Ace gone, he wouldn't have wasted time snitching. He'd have made sure Ace never got a chance to see another sunrise.

Like he intended to do the last time they crossed paths.

The thought settled in Ace's chest like a weight. He had survived that encounter – barely. But this? This was different. This was a setup, and he needed to figure out who was behind it before the walls closed in on him for good.

Ace had caught the drift the moment he and Whiteboy were ushered into that warehouse. Paul had played his hand masterfully, sending Ace on a mission he couldn't refuse – one designed to tap into his instincts, his hunger for revenge. But the energy in that warehouse had been undeniable. Paul wasn't just orchestrating moves; he was cleaning house, tying up any loose ends that could lead back to him.

The conversation with Stacey had peeled back layers Ace hadn't even realized existed. It had connected dots he hadn't thought to connect and raised new questions that filled his mind. But out of everything he'd learned that night, one detail refused to let go, gripping his thoughts like a pair of pliers.

Stacey had made one thing clear. She and her fellow agents were untouchable. Their lives weren't left to chance; they were protected by a debt – fifty million dollars' worth. That sum alone was enough to shift power dynamics enough to make men like Paul tread carefully. Yet Paul had ignored the supposed safety net, marking Stacey for death despite the apparent wishes of the real puppet master.

Gus.

That name had surfaced in their conversation, where she implied that the power, control, and authority went well beyond Paul's. Stacey had insisted that her survival was non-negotiable because it was tied to a larger game that went deeper than street politics. Yet there she was, dead at Paul's command.

So, what had changed?

Had Gus suddenly decided she was expendable, shifting the rules of engagement? Or had Paul gone rogue, making his own move without permission? If it was the latter, Ace had a feeling there would be consequences – the kind that could shake up everything, putting him right in the middle of the storm.

The latter seemed likely, which could explain why Paul had sent his henchmen to take out Whiteboy. Ace knew Paul had a big army of loyal soldiers, each one trained to handle anything that came their way. His reach was endless, and this alone made Paul an almost insurmountable force, far beyond what Ace could take on alone. The man was part of a powerful family with troops ready to execute orders in an instant.

Ace, on the other hand, had nothing. No backup. No safety net. All he had was his mind and the burning determination to keep moving forward. A direct confrontation with Paul would be suicide, and Ace knew it. Yet letting Paul get away with murdering his best friend? That was a line he couldn't allow anyone to cross and get away with. He clenched his fists, the thought of Whiteboy's death fueling a fire within him. He couldn't let it slide. He wouldn't.

He opened his eyes, and in the silence that followed, he let his thoughts settle. Paul had the power, the resources, the connections. But Ace wasn't entirely powerless. He had an angle. He could weaken

Paul's position by finding the stones and then tracking down Gus, the shadowy figure who loomed over everything. That seemed to be the only way. But first, he had to find Trigga. If he could locate him, he'd be one step closer to the answers he needed.

Yet amidst all this, his thoughts went back to Ariel. She was carrying their child, a life that belonged to them both. The weight of it felt like a blessing and a curse. He had already lost his first child, a wound so deep it had shaped every part of his existence. Now, here he was again, faced with a new life.

It couldn't have come at a worse time. He was on the run, surrounded by enemies, and barely holding his head together. Could he survive long enough to witness this child grow? If he was being honest with himself, he couldn't see it. The idea of a day where all this was behind him, where he could finally relax and raise a child, felt like a fantasy – too far-fetched to even entertain.

The weight of that realization settled in his chest, heavy and cold. Right now, he accepted that fate. Survival wasn't about a future anymore. It was about holding on just long enough to set things right.

He'd dug too deep into the hole to just rise and see the fresh fruits of dawn's light. At this point, he admitted to himself that he'd long passed the point of no return. The only way to atone for his actions now would likely come at the cost of his own life. A life of simplicity, of peace, would never be his reality. But even if it couldn't be his, he was determined to create it for Ariel and their unborn child.

A breath cascaded from his nostrils as the thought of his true purpose emerged from the shadows of obscurity. For the first time, the picture was clear; his role in life was meant to be a sacrifice for what was to come. All his selfish motives, all his choices made in pursuit of his own desires, would have to be amended with selflessness.

He thought back to the beginning, how every decision he made had been about what was better for him, never about what was better for the people who had built the foundation of his life. He had used all of them to satisfy his own agenda, and one by one, they'd paid the price. Everyone he'd failed was gone now, except Ariel.

Somehow, she had survived the chaos he'd created. She hadn't been slain in the reckless conquest of his own ambitions. Ariel had endured the weight of the burdens he had placed on her, standing strong where so many others had fallen. And he wouldn't let her crumble now. He wouldn't drag her down with him under the crushing pressure of his life.

Ace stood and walked over to the living room window, his gaze lifting to the sky. His eyes traced the outlines of the clouds as they drifted effortlessly across the atmosphere. *Damn*, he thought, *if only I could be free of all my problems like those clouds.*

He lingered there for a moment longer, staring at the beautiful, untouchable sky. Then, with a deep breath, a singular conclusion settled in his mind. He needed to find those diamonds – not for himself but for Ariel. She needed to be financially secure, able to care for their child without relying on the streets.

Once that was done, Ace knew what he'd become. He'd be a man with nothing to lose, and that would make him more dangerous than ever.

His days were already numbered, and Ace had resolved to spend what was left of them hunting down and killing everyone who had crossed him. In his mind, he'd mentally jolted down a list – a specific order of individuals who would answer for their wrongs against him.

Kero wasn't at the top. Ace had a bigger fish to fry, targets who would be harder to find and punish. But that didn't mean Kero was far from his thoughts. The lil nigga had put him in a losing predicament – one that ultimately led to Sassy's death.

Ace cared less about the *why* behind Kero's actions. The betrayal was all that mattered. Kero did what he did –period. And Ace would do what he had to in return. He had already mapped out the perfect payback – a plan so precise that it caused his pulse to quicken just by the mere thought of it.

Ace interlocked his fingers behind his head; his thoughts were heavy. If he was being honest with himself, he hated every bit of what he was about to do. But Kero's snake-ass actions had left no room for remorse. As Ace saw it, Kero had done everything in his power to ensure Ace's death. And, according to Stacey, Kero hadn't stopped there – he'd been aiming to go even further.

He couldn't rationalize it. There was no explanation that could make it make sense. Kero hadn't just betrayed him; he had personally fed him to the wolves.

Becoming increasingly agitated, Ace moved away from the window. *What's taking Ariel so long?* She was only supposed to grab a few clothes and the other small items he'd asked for. His eyes flicked to the clock on the coffee table again – two and a half hours had passed.

Ace tried to reassure himself. Ariel could handle herself; she'd proven that time and time again. But when he factored in the recent encounter with Paul's men at the hotel, the dynamic shifted. Ariel was strong. She'd handled more niggas than any woman Ace could think of, but those previous men weren't trained, disciplined killers.

The Italians were a different breed – dangerous, calculating, and ruthless. She wouldn't stand a chance against them, and the thought made his chest tighten. Ace nervously scratched at his forearm, stepping back toward the window. He couldn't afford to lose her.

He had to get her out of harm's way – for good.

It was nearly four hours before Ace could finally breathe a little easier. Ariel returned, bringing everything he'd asked for – and then some. She'd even taken the liberty of buying a worn-out, green jacket from some bum. Thoughtful, sure, but he figured he'd make it smell just as bad soon enough. Still, the stench made him question if he could even wear it.

Then there was the surprise, something he hadn't even thought to ask for. Under different circumstances, he'd swear she was trying to be funny. She'd picked up a dreaded wig and what looked like a patch of fake facial hair that might as well have been ripped off someone's face. He wanted to laugh out loud but held it back. Ace couldn't even imagine himself running around in this makeshift disguise, looking like a runaway slave. Then again, wasn't that exactly what he felt like at this point?

There were also two other things Ace never expected Ariel to think of on her own. She'd gone to his gunman, Tweety, and picked up a Glock .45 with two extended clips and a 3D-printed suppressor. How Tweety had managed to get his hands on a 3D silencer was beyond Ace, but he couldn't deny it would be perfect for his first stop.

Still, he remained skeptical. Tweety had told Ariel this was only the second one he'd ever handled, and it came with limitations. "No more than ten shots," Tweety had warned, "or it'll weaken and become useless."

Ace smirked to himself. Ten shots would be more than enough to handle Fanny.

By the time they finished discussing Ariel's reasons for all the extra items she'd bought – and every detail of what their next moves would be after tonight – the darkness of night had fully replaced the day. For the first time, they laid side by side without the presence of sexual intimacy or even the faintest hint of arousal.

Their bare skin touched, but their minds were miles apart. Ariel was consumed with thoughts of what should be, while Ace was singularly focused on what would be. The weight of reality had drawn an invisible line between them, their perspectives diverging in ways neither dared to acknowledge.

Somehow, Ace knew that only his success could bring them back to where they used to be.

Ace stared up at the darkened ceiling, his retinas locked in place as half of Ariel's body draped across his. The steady rhythm of her heartbeat seemed to sync with his, sending a surge of newfound motivation coursing through his veins, settling deep within his core.

Today wouldn't wait, and neither could he.

Easing out from under Ariel, Ace began putting on his disguise. The clothing was simple enough, but he'd need Ariel's help with the dreads and facial prosthetics. She had already warned him that the fake beard and eyebrows would start to come loose after about ten to twelve hours – and if he sweated too much, that timeline would shrink dramatically.

Ace made a mental note to keep the prosthetic adhesive within reach. The last thing he needed was for his disguise to fail at the worst possible moment, blowing his cover.

Once Ariel got out of bed, she helped him thoroughly wash his face before she stepped back and began carefully coaching him through each step of the process. Ace had wanted her to handle it, but she insisted he do it himself. After today, he wouldn't be able to depend on anyone but himself – a fact that he was already painfully aware of.

Standing in front of the bathroom mirror, Ace listened intently, meticulously following her instructions. His hands trembled slightly as he dabbed the prosthetic adhesive along his jawline, forcing himself to hold steady. After giving the solution a few minutes to set, he carefully placed and adjusted each piece of the facial disguise.

Next came the wig cap. With a little assistance from Ariel, the dreadlock wig was aligned perfectly with the smooth fibers of the cap and secured in place with bobby pins.

After a few final touches, Ace stared at the unbelievable reflection in the mirror. He had transformed himself into someone else entirely and was amazed by how convincing the disguise looked. His face now resembled that of an older man, rugged and unkempt. The synthetic brows and beard matched his hair perfectly, blending seamlessly with the rest of his features. The uneven twists of the coarse dreadlocks fell over his shoulders, mimicking years of neglect and adding an air of authenticity.

Ace couldn't help but smile as Ariel fluffed the dreads with her fingers, adjusting them to fall just right. When she was done, he leaned in close to the mirror, his eyes scanning every outline and detail for any flaws. For a full minute, he inspected his newly attached features in silence.

Finally, he slapped his hands on the counter, a grin spreading across his face. The outcome exceeded his expectations. Not only was he unrecognizable, but the disguise also gave him an invaluable advantage. Ace glanced at Ariel, gratitude shining in his eyes. Her thoughtfulness had given him the edge he desperately needed.

Turning to her, he gripped her waist and pulled her close. As their eyes met, Ace felt a wave of appreciation well up inside him. He wished he had the time to show her, in a thousand different ways, how much he was indebted to her. But deep down, he knew there was only one way she truly wanted to be thanked.

And he'd use every fiber and muscle in his body to make it count.

"Once I get the paper from Kero's sis, I'ma bring that for you to leave with. Then, I'm going to find them muthafucking diamonds.

When I get them, I'm coming straight to you, A. After that, we – *together* – can decide the next chapter in our life. Whatever you wanna do, I'm with it. You done stood by me more than enough times to deserve that and…"

"Shhh," Ariel placed her index finger on his lips. "Bae, we've stood by each other and gone continue to through whatever. That's how it's been and how it will always be. But right now, I don't need you to think bout our future – or me. I need you to focus on taking it to these muthafuckas in the worst way. Kill 'em all and kill any nigga that try to stop you." Ariel touched both sides of his face. "Right now, that's all I need from you – what we need from you," she said softly before leaning in to kiss him, careful not to disturb the delicate constructs of his disguise. Ariel's love for Ace was immeasurable but love alone couldn't shield her from reality.

Last night, she had been forced to confront every realistic outcome Ace might face, and truth be told, none of them were results she could easily live with. Yet there was one she might eventually come to terms with because, in the end, he'd still be alive.

But Ariel knew Ace too well. He'd never – willingly – accept such a fate. His nature was too rebellious, too defiant to be controlled by anything other than the desires of his own heart. Last night, she had come to grips with that truth because, deep down, she understood.

He had to face this head-on, and he needed to be relentlessly focused if he was going to emerge victorious in the king's game.

Ace had felt every part of what she'd said, and there wasn't anything for him to say in response. He would do whatever it took to see his seed born. There existed no other choice.

Later that evening, Ace gathered everything he'd need to accomplish his first mission. Ariel had drove an hour before dropping him off within walking distance of Kero's sister's apartment, which was located in East Point.

CHAPTER SIX

Louis Gram

"Mmm-mmh," Gram huffed, taking down the last bite of the Baja Chipotle Turkey sandwich. After the brief exchange with Senator Peters, he thought it best to grab something to eat before he made his grand entrance into the *Wilkins Primary Task Force* headquarters.

There was no telling when the next time he'd be allowed to enjoy a meal. He was about to step into a pool of all types of clashes between political agendas, departmental pride, and personal vendettas. It was the kind of case that could make or break a career – or worse, get someone killed.

Tossing the sandwich wrapper in the nearest trash can, Gram stepped out of his car then made his way into the Atlanta Police Department Headquarters. Swiping his visitor's badge at the checkpoint, he then made his way to the elevator. As the doors slid open, he stepped inside and pressed the button for the fourth floor.

The ride was quiet, giving him a brief moment to gather his thoughts. Two days ago, he'd never heard Sophia Williams' name. Now, he was leading the taskforce investigating her murder. He knew the game. There were forces at play beyond just street criminals. And he hated being dropped in the middle of a mess without knowing who the grand chef was that was stirring the brew.

The elevator chimed, and the doors slid open to reveal a hallway lined with offices and workstations. At the end, there was the door with *Wilkins Primary Task Force* etched on the front, which led to the headquarters of the new unit. Gram pushed through, entering.

Inside, the taskforce office was already buzzing with movement. Detectives hunched over files, and analysts typed away on keyboards, the low murmur of conversations filling the space. The large digital evidence board dominated the rear of the room, flickering with the limited information they had on Sophia's murder.

Gram cleared his throat, getting everyone's attention. "Alright, listen up. I'm Louis Gram. *None* of you know me, but this is what all of you need to know. I'm running this taskforce now, and I don't plan on doing anything besides catching those responsible for the murder of DEA Special Agent Sophia Williams."

He glanced around a moment, letting the severity of it hang in the air. "She was one of us, and this case will be treated with your highest regards. There will be no screw-up, no leaks, no egos. The FBI, the DEA, and APD – *we* are all working this thing together whether we like it or not.

"I've read what we've got so far, and to be honest, it's not much. But there are two suspects, Anthony Jackson and Michael Turner." Gram pointed at the pictures on the digital screen. "These two were flagged by an anonymous tip. We don't have anything solid on them yet. The surveillance footage from the mall and the surrounding area will be reviewed over in case a small detail was looked over. These two men are still on the loose, and that's a problem."

He let that sink in before moving from person to person to see who they were and their actual job description.

"Okay, McCarthy, I want you working the tip – who made the call, where it came from, and if it smells even remotely legit, chase it down. Walker, pull every record we have on Jackson and Turner – associates, priors, anything that says something about them. And see if there's *anything* that connects them to Sophia."

The room stirred as everyone moved into action. Gram exhaled, rubbing his jaw as he turned toward the evidence board. He studied the images they had. It was a few pictures of grainy footage of Sophia at the mall, strategically moving between stores, checking her phone every few seconds. But there was nothing from the moment she was shot – no images of the killers, no indication of where the two came from in the attack.

"That doesn't make any damn sense," he muttered to himself, his eyes scanning the screen a second time.

"You're right. It doesn't."

The unexpected voice made him turn. A short, Asian woman stood beside him, arms crossed, watching the same images.

"And you are?" Gram asked, already annoyed by the interruption of the small woman.

She smirked slightly. "Stephanie Towns. DEA. Your new partner, *Detective* Louis Gram."

Gram barely concealed his irritation. "Mmh." He exhaled through his nose, looking her up and down. The last thing he needed was a *small* person from another agency breathing down his neck. But from the way she held her posture, he could already tell she thought of herself as a tough ass.

Towns smirked. Gram's irritation was obvious. With her arms still crossed, she tilted her head slightly. "Not a fan of the DEA, huh? Or is it just the way you treat pretty women?"

Gram exhaled sharply, shaking his head. "I'm not a fan of having federal watch dogs assigned to my ass. Regardless if they're pretty or not."

Towns raised an eyebrow. "Oh, God, please don't tell me *he's* one of those types?"

"Exactly that type," Gram huffed, reaching for the file the chief had given him. "But since I'm stuck with the *pretty woman*, how about she file the formal request? I want to *re*-interview Swift, Stell, and their latest edition." Gram searched the file quickly with his index finger. "Justin Kirkland." He leaned in slightly, lowering his voice with a smirk. "You can manage that, *pretty girl?* Since you're not just here for moral support."

Towns' eyes narrowed, but her smirk didn't fade. "I think I can handle that. Paperwork's kind of our thing, you know? Right after ruining local law enforcement's day."

Gram gave a sarcastic chuckle. "I do believe that's correct. You guys are like taxes. Nobody asks for you, but we're stuck dealing with you anyway."

Towns pretended to be impressed. "Wow. Cop humor. You guys still using the same jokes from the 90s, or do you mix it up sometimes?"

Gram shrugged. "Hey, if it ain't broke…" He stepped back, giving her a gesture toward the front table. "Go on then. Handle that request. When you're done, we're heading to the crime scene. Might as well see where the ghosts of this case are hiding."

Towns shook her head, pulling up the request form on the laptop. "This is gonna be a long ass case, isn't it?"

Gram grinned as he leaned against the doorway. "Oh, no doubt. Hope you've packed a briefcase."

CHAPTER SEVEN

Freshman Black

"You'd think niggas would move more cautious after knowing there were niggas out there ready to change the way they were living their lives." Freshman stared out the window at the barbershop which set at least forty yards away from them. The time was eleven-forty a.m. Him and Hot had been parked at the small, six building plaza for almost twenty minutes, waiting to see the nigga, Lonzo.

Freshman had agreed to meet Lonzo around four o'clock to discuss the role he'd play in helping Freshman reclaim his rightful spot. But trust? That wasn't something Freshman handed out lightly. He didn't trust any nigga enough to blindly walk into one of their traps.

Lonzo was still in the Hand, which meant he could easily be playing the part just to get Freshman caught up. And Freshman didn't have time for the fuck-me games. That was why he had to catch Lonzo off guard.

He needed Lonzo – just not because he'd acquired real influence in the Hand but because of his position. Lonzo was the one who coordinated most of the everyday movements of transactions. He was the glue that kept operations running smoothly. Live had already told Freshman that Tip had promoted Lonzo to *Handler,* a position Freshman himself had once filled.

Freshman knew that, as the *Handler*, Lonzo had access to everyone, something that would make this transition a whole lot easier.

He glanced over at Hot, who'd been unusually quiet for most of the drive and the stakeout. Freshman figured he was in a mood. He still hadn't made it to the same page of how Freshman wanted to handle things with Lonzo. Hot had made his opinion clear earlier, arguing that pulling up on Lonzo like this was risky and unnecessary.

Freshman felt otherwise. Of course, he felt like Lonzo was a little too unpredictable to trust his word alone. That was why he chose to get a real read on him by catching him off guard. That was Freshman's style – head-on, no guessing games.

Hot, on the other hand, preferred killing them and taking what they had. Freshman could tell by his tight-lipped silence that Hot was biting his tongue. Still, Freshman wasn't about to press the issue. They'd been through too much together for Hot to doubt where his mind was at.

Hot continued to stare out the windshield, his gaze sharp and watchful. Despite the tension, Freshman knew one thing for certain. Hot had his back.

The tension in the air was thick, and Freshman couldn't ignore it. "You good?" he asked, breaking the silence.

Hot's head turned slightly, but his expression remained unreadable. "Yeah, I'm good," he said flatly, though the edge in his voice suggested otherwise. Freshman let it slide for now, knowing that their next move with Lonzo would speak louder than any words they could exchange.

Freshman and Hot sat in the vehicle. Hot tapped his fingers on the steering wheel, his eyes flickering between the barbershop and the rest of the outside world. He was deliberately avoiding Freshman's gaze. Then, just as Hot was about to open his mouth to speak, the shop's door swung open, and Lonzo stepped out into the sun's rays.

"Boom. There he go," Freshman muttered, leaning forward slightly.

Lonzo was nonchalantly strolling to his car, oblivious of the pairs of eyes watching his every move. He slid into the driver's seat, started the engine, and pulled out of the parking lot.

Hot waited until Lonzo got a good distance before easing the car onto the street, keeping enough distance to avoid tipping him off. Losing him wasn't a concern though — the white van with *Rug Cleaner* decals had already pulled out ahead of them, carrying the four-man hit team Hot had assembled.

The idea of putting together a squad had come up days ago, and Hot immediately knew the right guys for the job. They weren't former members or friends of the Hand, which meant Freshman didn't have to worry about loyalty conflicts or hidden agendas. These were men motivated solely by money, and Hot had promised them plenty once the plan succeeded.

Freshman regretted not having the chance to fully vet each member of the team himself, but the plan had come together on short notice. Still, he trusted Hot's judgment, and if Hot said these guys were solid, that was good enough for him. Hot had handled everything – the men, the van, and the logistics. Now, Freshman would see just how well this crew could execute under pressure.

This wasn't just a test for Lonzo; it was a test for the team.

During the pursuit, the car remained silent except for Hot muttering instructions into his phone to the team in the van. Freshman had been clear about the plan – he just wanted them to wait for the signal to act, which would come when the time was right.

They trailed Lonzo through a few turns, weaving effortlessly through light traffic. Each twist and turn brought them closer to their moment of action. Finally, they found themselves on a quiet two-lane street, the road nearly deserted with only a handful of cars in sight.

Freshman glanced at the side mirror and smirked. "Showtime."

With Lonzo two cars away from the red light, the van swerved alongside him. As it matched his speed, the side door slid open, and the barrel of an assault rifle emerged, aimed squarely at him. It only took a split second for Lonzo's face to twist into shock.

His first instinct was to hit the gas, but the cars in front of him at the light made that impossible. The option immediately left his mind. Panic began to set in as the reality of the situation sank in – there was no way out.

"Nigga, unlock the fucking doors!" He heard the dude scream with a menacing glare in his eyes. Lonzo waited another second before complying. He'd hoped the light would have changed to green by now. His luck, it was still red.

"Unlock the doors now!" the man barked again, this time setting his aim steady like he was ready to shoot.

Lonzo's retinas darted between the rifle and his rearview mirror where he saw someone with a hoodie on step out of a vehicle somewhere behind his. He cursed under his breath, assuming this was a carjacking. With a reluctant sigh, he hit the unlock button.

Swiftly, Freshman moved with his head down to Lonzo's rear door, yanked it open, and slid in quickly. "Drive, nigga," Freshman said coldly, pressing the barrel of his pistol into Lonzo's side. "We finally get to talk face to face." With that, Freshman pulled the hoodie from his head, so Lonzo could see his face.

Lonzo's eyes bulged as his face turned even paler from shock. "Pee? Nigga, what the fuck is this? We sa…"

"Nigga, just drive," Freshman repeated. His voice became calm, yet there was still a touch of aggression riding it. "Focus on the road. We'll talk somewhere else."

After ten minutes of turning and going through various streets, Lonzo finally found a quiet side street and pulled over, parking next to the curb. His knuckles were white on the steering wheel, his body tense as though bracing for whatever came next.

In contrast, Freshman sat in the backseat like an Uber passenger who'd just reached his destination. He leaned back casually with a smirk tugging at the corner of his lips. He looked around the empty street, nodding in approval, as if satisfied with Lonzo's service.

"Good spot," Freshman muttered, finally breaking the silence. He leaned forward slightly, his voice taking on a dangerous edge. "Now, fuck why I pulled up on you like this. You already know I don't like wasting time – are you with me or against me?"

Lonzo shifted uncomfortably in his seat, his eyes flicking nervously to the rearview mirror to meet Pee Pee's calm but deadly gaze. "Freshman, you already know a nigga with you. Hell, I'm the one who told Live to hit you, nigga, remember?"

Freshman shifted slightly at the mention of the nickname. It had been christened by Black in front of most of the Hand during a grand event at the Hilton hotel ballroom. The night was electric. Black had thrown the gathering to celebrate the accomplishments of his comrades and to commemorate Mal for everything he'd helped build.

It had been two weeks since Mal's death and only three days since his burial. Black was still on edge, grappling with the loss of his brother. But in his mind, the best way to honor Mal was to push forward in a way that he knew Mal would have wanted.

An hour into the celebration, Black, who was overly lit, took to the stage with a Moscato bottle in hand. His words were slurred slightly into the microphone as he dedicated heartfelt sentiments to Mal and spoke of his love for the Hand. Then, as if struck by a sudden thought, Black paused mid-sentence. The room fell silent as he stood there, the luminescent lights casting a glow over him, giving him an almost god-like aura.

With the bottle dangling at his side, Black scanned the room before speaking again. He declared that the time for mourning would also be a time for moving forward – a display of strength in the face of tragedy, and to emphasize his point, he called Pee Pee to the stage.

Black's words were few but impactful. He introduced Pee Pee as the leader of the new members and an example for those who weren't. It was a defining moment, one that solidified Pee Pee's place in the family – and one he would never forget.

In Black's words that night, Pee Pee had earned every bit of what was bound to him as Black's Hand. He was to be the living embodiment of Black's principles, and in Black's drunken eyes, he seemed exactly that. It was then that Black christened him with the name "Freshman Black."

At first, *Freshman* had come to hate the title, mainly because of the countless jokes and snide remarks made by his fellow brothers whenever Black's back was turned. Even though he was second in command, the position often felt like he was nothing more than Black's errand boy, jumping whenever the 'good little boy' was told to.

One time, he'd come close to shooting a brother in the face over the ongoing taunts. But that very moment was the turning point for him. That was when he learned to accept the fact that he was in his position because he'd been better at this life than the rest of them were.

From then on, he stopped letting the name bother him. Instead, he owned it, letting the name stick, here and there, because it no longer carried the weight of shame and regret.

The corners of his mouth curved into a faint smirk. The mentioning of the nickname brought his purpose sharply into focus. Every memory, every trial, every step that had led him here began to crystallize within his mind.

Freshman nodded his head. "That's respectful." He sat back in the seat, looking at Lonzo, thinking that he had chose the right way to acknowledge his leadership. Resting the pistol on his knee, he asked Lonzo, "Ight, so tell me how you finna help me sit upon the throne?"

Lonzo's eyes found Freshman's in the rearview mirror. "By helping you knock Tip off of it. Bra, niggas knew that soon as you came back into the picture, how this shit was supposed to go. But it's only a few of us who believe in that…"

"And still a nigga ain't did shit about it," Freshman said, cutting in. Though quickly, he reminded himself that he wasn't here to examine niggas' reasons for failing to uphold the code. This meeting held two purposes, and he was about to attain both. "But that's old news. We here to create the new. I want you to prove to me that we on the same page. You the *Handler,* right?"

Lonzo nodded his head. "Yeah."

Freshman stared out the window, his voice calm yet laced with menace. "Good. Then you already know what's next. Tip needs to fall, but first, I need to break the morale of his followers. Bo showed me just how deeply rooted his influence has become. Let me see your phone."

Lonzo hesitated for a moment, his hand hovering before finally picking up and unlocking the phone. Slowly, he lifted his gaze to the rearview mirror, holding the device backward for Freshman to take.

"Now, where's the Handler's phone?" Freshman asked, taking the device. His eyes narrowed, studying Lonzo carefully. He wondered did his move with the one phone need to be taken as a minor mistake or a deliberate gesture of stupidity. Time would tell.

Lonzo chewed on the skin on his bottom lip, as if he was undecided about his next action. Yet being indecisive wasn't the issue. He needed a full understanding of what his position would be after he aided in Freshman's ascent to the top. The Handler spot was one of the best places a nigga could be in, though that was still below the spot he felt his feet belonged in.

"So, what's my situation gonna look like after *we* put you on the throne?" Without breaking eye contact, he reached into the narrow space between his seat and the center console. A moment later, he pulled out a small, black, flip phone and held it in the air, offering it to Freshman like a bargaining chip.

Freshman leaned forward, studying Lonzo. "What exactly you mean by your situation?" His voice carried the weight of expectation.

Lonzo moved uncomfortably in his seat, glancing briefly at the flip phone in Freshman's hand. "I mean, once you back in charge, where that leave me? I ain't looking to stay where I'm at, Fresh. You already know a nigga in this shit all the way."

Freshman smirked, sitting back as he casually flipped through the phone's contacts. "Aight. I hear you," he said, his tone giving just enough acknowledgment without fully agreeing. "But here's the thing, Lonzo – today? Today ain't about no promises. Today is about you turning in your application. You wanna be my right hand? Then you gotta show me you worth it."

As he scrolled through the list of contacts, Freshman noticed something peculiar: every name in the phone was abbreviated into two – or three – letter arrangements. His brows furrowed slightly before stopping at "MO". He held the phone up, his voice tinged with curiosity. "Who this? MO?"

"That's Mook," Lonzo replied quickly.

"Mook?" Freshman repeated, watching Lonzo's reaction carefully. "What he about?"

Lonzo hesitated for a split second before answering. "He was one of Tip's lil soldiers, then he got his big promotion. Bra a Tip fan."

Freshman's jaw tightened, and his expression darkened. "Tip fan, huh? Aight. So, where you think this nigga at right now?"

Lonzo exhaled through his nose. "More than likely," he paused, glancing at Freshman, "he's probably posted up at one of his spots. Could be the lil studio over on Hemphill."

"Hemphill? Never heard of it but let's pull up on 'em. You got time?" Pee Pee smirked. Then, he called a number in his phone. After a ring, Hot picked up.

"Aye, change of plans. Make sure the lil ones all the way ready to handle this new business." Freshman was already aware that they'd been strapped to help with Lonzo. He now thought of something that would definitely send a message to the core of the Hand. Lonzo said there were a few who felt that he should be in his rightful position. So, he felt that the time was ripe to correct those who didn't.

Freshman listened to Hot's reply then said, "Cool, have them follow us. And tell them be ready." He ended the call. Lonzo turned over the ignition, and Freshman began to stare a hole into the side of his head. How prepared was Lonzo to see this through? He was ready to find out.

It took Lonzo twenty minutes to finally make it to Hemphill Avenue where he parked at a safe distance from the group gathered in front of the small studio. Without any hesitation, Lonzo pointed out Mook – a tall, dark-skinned nigga draped in a few pieces of jewelry who rocked a swamp green outfit.

Mook stood among a few others in front of the place, smoking and talking, very unaware of the eyes now locked on him.

Freshman dialed Hot. As soon as he answered, Freshman laid out the plan, breaking down exactly how he wanted things to unfold once he gave the signal. With that handled, he called Mook.

Down the street, Freshman watched as Mook casually put a blunt to his lips while fishing the phone out of his pocket. A moment later, he answered.

"Yo, what up, Zo?" Mook answered.

"This Pee Pee, nigga…" From a distance, Freshman watched Mook's reaction. The line went silent. The only sound coming through was the background chatter. Then, Mook lifted a hand for those around him to be quiet.

"The fuck you calling me for, nigga? Where Lonzo?" Mook's demeanor instantly turned aggressive. Freshman could tell that he'd put the phone on speaker for all of them to hear.

"Shid, he around," Freshman began with light chuckle, "and since you put me on speaker, I'ma address you and whoever else the fuck around you. I'm giving niggas one chance to stick to the code Black put down. If nig…"

Mook cut him off before he could finish. "Nigga, Black dead…"

Freshman listened as one of the people to the left of him leaned over Mook's shoulder and said, "And so is you, nigga!"

"Say no more," was the only response Freshman gave before disconnecting the call. Quickly, he called Hot, saying, "Wipe 'em."

"I told you the nigga was a Tip fan," Lonzo said, about to turn over the ignition until Freshman stopped him.

"Yeah, but I'm all for the family, so I gotta give niggas a chance to make the right decision."

Both Freshman and Lonzo watched as the *Rug Cleaner* van rolled past them, slowing as it reached the intersection. Making a left, it pulled up on the side of the studio, idling in place.

Meanwhile, Mook and his entourage remained at the front, completely unfazed, as if Freshman's words hadn't bothered them in the least. And he was cool with that. In fact, he was grateful – because it meant they wouldn't sense what was coming.

Now, he'd get to watch the spectacle unfold exactly as planned.

The van's side door slid open, and the three men hopped out, assault rifles in hand. Freshman leaned over the middle console, his eyes narrowing as he watched them move. The trio crept along the side of the building, their movements sharp and precise.

Then, the gunfire erupted.

A smirk tugged at the corners of Freshman's mouth as the shooters hit the corner fast, unleashing relentless gunfire. The group in the front didn't even have a chance to scatter – bullets tore through them before they could react.

Mook was the first to drop, his body twisting as the barrage of rounds trampled him into the pavement.

In mere seconds, the entire entourage was sprawled across the ground, covered in gore and smoldering flesh.

As the trio retreated back to the van, Freshman kept his eyes locked on the scene. Everything became still; every sign of life was gone.

Then, from the studio's front door, someone cautiously peeked out, hesitating before taking a step.

Freshman fell back in his seat, his gaze settling on Lonzo's emotionless face. "Preciate the ride, my nigga. Make sure you hit me later on, so we can keep speeding this process up, aight?" As he spoke, he caught sight of Hot's car pulling up beside them.

Lonzo's eyes found Freshman's in the rearview mirror. "Cool, but I want my position, Pee."

Freshman smiled, grabbing the door handle as he slid across the seat. "When we get to that bridge. And from here on, call me Freshman Black."

Jumping in the car with Hot, Freshman held up his index finger, signaling Hot to wait as he was about to say something. He quickly scrolled through the phone to the letter he'd saved the contact under. Then, his thumb tapped the call icon.

After two rings, Tip answered. "Who this?"

"It's Pee, nigga. You still ain't reconsidered?"

"Dirty, reconsider what? That move you pulled on Bo got niggas heated and ready to lay yo head before my feet." Tip chuckled, amused.

"Yeah, I heard that much from Mook and them. And we see how that turned out." It was now Freshman's turn to be amused. He looked beyond the window at the sprawled bodies as they passed, wondering how long it would take the news to reach Tip's ears.

"Nigga, what?" Tip sounded lost.

"You bout to get a call." With that, Freshman disconnected. Tip said that *niggas* were heated bout Bo. He could only imagine how furious they'd get in response to Mook, and the crews' fall out.

All of which he needed. Emotions in any form were known to easily cloud people's judgment, which damn near always subjected them to fatal mistakes – something he planned to take advantage of.

CHAPTER EIGHT

Ace

"I love you…" Ace said to Ariel, checking himself out one more time. The ride had taken somewhere close to an hour, and he was confident that no one would ever think he was the guy on every news channel in the nation.

He walked as if life wasn't going anywhere anytime soon. Ace finally made it to a liquor store, purchasing a small bottle of gin. Gulping a sip, he waited until he was sure no eyes were on him and dabbed some on his clothing before tossing the bottle. He knew at the pace he moved that it would take him at least ten to fifteen minutes to make it to the River Bank apartments. Building E was a good distance from the front of the apartment complex, so he knew an extra few minutes was part of his journey.

Months ago, Kero had moved his younger sibling – *Fanny* – out here to get her out of their crackhead mother's deteriorated house and away from the hood where everyone knew them. Fanny was a real reflection of her mother – ages before she'd become addicted to the glass dick. She was shorter than her brother, and her skin was a beautiful jet-black, which was darker than both her mother's and brother's skin.

But like any so-called brother would, he asked Ace to help him move her belongings. Had it been anybody else, Ace would have turned him down. But it was Kero and Fanny, who he considered to be blood. So, he helped and visited a couple of times.

At this very moment, he was glad he had because he couldn't think of anyone else in the world who Kero gave two fucks about enough to trust to keep a portion of his bread.

Now that he thought about it, Ace wondered if Kero remembered that he knew Fanny's whereabouts. It was possible Kero had smartly moved her and her three-year-old child out of harm's way.

Of course, Kero had plenty of sense, but Ace doubted he had enough to predict his next move. One thing was certain. Kero knew that once Ace found out about his betrayal, revenge was inevitable. Moving Fanny would've been a logical step.

However, Ace had one advantage. He was a wanted man. That alone might've led Kero to believe he was out of the picture, no longer a threat worth worrying about. And Ace was betting on that.

Ace continued forward until he spotted The River Banks Apartments green and white sign. His eyes darted across the area, scanning for anyone who might see him turn off toward the right. A thick line of trees stretched from the sidewalk down behind the buildings, forming a shield. The space between the tree line and the apartment complex was narrow, *too* tight for anything besides kids playing hide-and-seek. It was a perfect cover.

Moving cautiously, Ace weaved between the trees, his eyes flicking to each building's assigned letter. He remembered Fanny had moved into Building E, but the exact apartment number escaped him. That didn't matter. Once he stood in front of E-2, he'd know which door was hers.

He slowed his pace as the distant sounds of laughter met his ears. A child's giggles. Then, a woman's voice could be heard from around the corner in the front of the complex.

Ace's heartbeat quickened. He lightened his step, inching forward, muscles tense. Peeking around the corner, he saw them. His breath caught. Fate was playing its hand.

Fanny sat on the edge of a faded green bench just outside the apartment building, one leg crossed over the other, lazily watching her three-year-old son push a plastic dump truck through the dirt.

She held a phone to her ear, laughing at something coming from the other end. Her attention was half on the conversation, half on the child.

Little Josh, completely into his activity, scooped up handfuls of gravel and poured it into the toy's open bed. He had no idea the world around him held any danger. Neither did his mother.

Ace crouched a little as he crept along from the side of the building, his steps calculated, his heartbeat steady despite the weight of what he was about to do. The oversized jacket hung loosely from his frame, dirt-streaked and sagging like it belonged to a man who had lost everything. A tattered beanie was pulled low over his dreads, shadowing his face.

To anyone passing by, he was just another homeless man shuffling through the complex, searching for shelter. But Ace wasn't here for rest.

His gaze locked onto Fanny, her carefree laughter grating against his nerves. She had no idea how close she was to the end.

He took a slow breath, steadying himself. No hesitation. No turning back.

Staying out of her sight for a moment, Ace watched. Then, he moved forward a little.

Fanny's posture was relaxed, but not entirely. He knew her too well to miss the subtle tells – how she shifted every so often, how her fingers absently picked at a thread on her jeans, how her gaze flickered toward the parking lot entrance every few minutes. She wasn't expecting trouble. But she was expecting something.

Perfect.

Ace stepped forward just enough to slip into her peripheral vision, his movements slow, unhurried, like he had nowhere else to be.

At first, she barely noticed him, just another homeless man, a background figure in the daily rhythm of life. Her focus was split between the conversation in her ear and her son, who attempted to babble something about his toy. She nodded absently, brushing a stray hair from her face. Then – a pause.

Her body stiffened with the tiniest hitch in her breath. She turned her head slightly, her eyes flicking to him for half a second before shifting away. But that half-second was enough. Ace saw it – the moment her brain caught up, the moment some realization set in.

And just like that, the tension in the air became more than evident.

Then Ace spoke. "Fanny."

Her entire body went rigid. She turned her head slowly, eyes narrowing as she took him in. Her lips parted slightly. "Do I know you?"

He took another step forward, the sun hitting his face just enough for her to get a better look at him. Maybe she'd recognize him beneath the disguise. He put his index finger to his mouth. "It's me – Ace."

Fanny inhaled sharply, forcing herself to stay still as she hung up the phone abruptly. *Don't panic. Don't let him see that you know.*

"Ace? How…" she said, her voice measured and calm, but he could hear the slight tremor beneath it.

Ace smirked slightly, tilting his head. "I had to think quick. I know you saw the news?"

Fanny swallowed hard. She reached for her son instinctively and pulled him to her in a protective manner.

"Yeah, I did," she confirmed, her tone shaky, but she was trying to keep it steady. "But why are you here? You pose to be halfway across the world," she said, chuckling uneasily.

Ace took a slow step closer, his eyes never leaving hers. "Have you talked to Kero? He suppose to be meeting me out here to give me a lil going away gift. I lost everything," he said, closely watching her body language.

Fanny's jaw tightened as her eyebrows furrowed. "He told you to meet him out here? He didn't say anything to me about it."

Ace glanced down at the kid then back up at her, keeping his expression unreadable. "Damn, we talked not too long ago. You already know how he be getting caught up, but shit, call him. And I know the lil disguise is crazy, but why you acting so edgy like this ain't me, *Baby Girl?*"

He called her the name she'd been used to him calling her. Ace was the most wanted man in America right now, so Fanny's awkward vibe was reasonably justified. But he wanted a real *tell-tell* reaction from her, something to confirm whether she was nervous for a reason or just thrown off by his sudden appearance.

Either way, he needed to get inside of her apartment, hopefully unnoticed. Yet, if she'd been forewarned and was about to do some stupid shit to cause a scene, he'd shoot her dead right here and take his chances.

Hell, he'd taken a chance by coming out here, and look how things were working out so far. He was all *in*.

A small smirk appeared on her lips, and her pulse pounded in her ears, but she forced herself to keep his gaze, refusing to let him see the fear tearing at her insides.

"Acey, you know it ain't even like that. But your face is everywhere…" Her voice lowered. "They talking bout you killed that police lady. I don't wanna get caught up in that." Positioning her son between her legs, she moved her fingers along the screen of the phone a second then placed it to her ear.

Ace took a quick glance around the scenery while she was distracted. He was grateful that nothing about the setting had changed besides her frantically moving fingers after Kero missed her call. He began to wonder how many chances he could take.

Wrapping his fingers tightly around the handle, Ace swiftly took three long steps, closing the space between them. Fanny's body jerked to the left, her knees tightening around the baby, but she didn't move from her seat. A gasp left her lips. Ace whipped out the weapon before a sound could leave her throat.

"I see he told you. Get the fuck up," Ace growled, making the gun and suppressor visible.

Terrified, Fanny began to plead. "Please, Ace, don't do this." Kero's words rang in her head. *Ace tried to set me up.*

At the time, she thought it was crazy. Ace was like the big brother they never had. Yeah, he and Kero had their issues, but it had never escalated to a point where she was caught in the middle. And now? Now she stood frozen, clutching her child, staring down the barrel of a gun held by someone she had always seen as blood.

"Blame Kero," Ace muttered, his voice cold. With a light grip, he grabbed the back of her neck as she lifted her child into her arms.

He hated that it had come to this – hated that he had to do this to someone he saw as a little sister. But Kero had forfeited all his love for anyone carrying his blood. And now, Fanny was just another casualty in the war Kero started.

"What he do?" she asked, her voice trembling as her eyes darted around, frantically searching for anyone who could help. To her disappointment, the entire area was lifeless – just her, Josh, and Ace. No one and no escape.

Her grip tightened around her three-year-old, her arms shielding him like a precious jewel. Her eyes glazed over, panic creeping in. She had no idea what her next move should be, but one thing was clear – she had to get the love of her life out of harm's way.

She had known Ace for years, had trusted him. She couldn't picture him actually hurting them. But she never thought he'd pull a gun on her either. And now, he had.

Ace guided her toward the stairs. "Something that's unforgivable, Fanny. But me and him gonna deal with that. Right now, I need that money he stashed over here, and this a be over, ight? I know it's fucked up, and I feel fucked up bout doing this. Kero left me no choice though."

Ace watched her closely as they moved up the stairwell. He noticed that due to little Josh being actively in her arms, she couldn't fumble around on the phone's screen. This was a good thing because he'd taken the risk of letting her call him the first time. That hadn't been part of the plan, but then again, her sitting out on the bench hadn't been either.

Fanny didn't respond right away. Her mind drifted back for a moment, replaying the last time Kero had come over.

The other day, he'd been different – amped about something when she let him in. His energy was off; his movements were restless, like he was riding a high that had nothing to do with drugs. She remembered how he paced her living room, talking in half-finished thoughts, barely letting her get a word in.

At the time, she brushed it off as Kero being Kero. Now, standing here with Ace, his gun weighing down the moment, she wondered had that been a warning sign that something more was at hand. Fanny was more than aware of some of the things Ace and her brother were involved in, so she knew that whatever had happened was serious.

"Okay, Ace, I'ma give you the money. Just please leave me and my baby out of whatever y'all got going on." Fanny stopped in front of her apartment door, hesitating, as if waiting for some kind of confirmation – some sign that he'd let them walk away from this untouched.

She had the combination to the safe he'd placed over here when she first moved in. That wasn't a problem, but the second one?

Her pulse quickened. A couple of days ago, Kero had brought in another safe that was a tad bigger than the first and said, "This one ain't to be touched. Period." He hadn't even looked at her when he said it. Just left it sitting there like it was a secret that could ruin everything.

Now, standing here with Ace at her back, she wondered if there was money inside – or something worse. And if she told Ace about it, would he let her and Josh go?

She swallowed hard, gripping her son a little tighter, praying Ace would take the thousands the safe offered and walk away. Quite obviously, whatever had gone down between them was beyond their regular fall outs.

Turning the knob, Fanny pushed the door open and stepped in with Ace on her heels. The TV was the only sound to be heard throughout the apartment. Ace swept his eyes around the interior as he shut the door and gestured for Fanny to sit. She did and sat baby Josh next to her. With one swift kick of the legs, he was off the couch.

"No, Josh…" Fanny said in tears.

Ace stared at her a moment. This was a girl he'd grown to love, and the tears that were beginning to spew down her face wasn't helping in justifying his actions. But again, this was Kero's fault, and he'd left him no room to even think about sympathy. So, he would be responsible for everything that was about to occur.

Little Josh began to loudly protest his mother's hindering, then Ace spoke. "Fanny, call Kero again…"

"If-if you want the money, I-I can give it to you now," Fanny told him through her sobs while trying to calm her child down.

"I'ma let you get it in a sec. Call Kero again. He needs to know that I'm here." The child wailed on the couch, as Fanny called again. After

Ace realized she still didn't get an answer, he told her to text him that this was an emergency. He'd known Kero for years, so him missing an urgent phone call was nothing new. And most likely, it was the same thing which had kept him from answering them – pussy.

Ace slightly shook his head. Kero had picked the wrong time to be somewhere fucking off with his sister's life on... Damn, he couldn't think because little Josh was trying his best to burst both of their ear drums. "Fanny, please let that boy get down?" he asked, becoming irritated by the obnoxious screaming.

Fanny looked at him as more tears ran down her face. "Ace, I don't know who you is right now."

"Well, can you get him a bottle or something? Damn!" Ace looked at the boy and was about to move toward the kitchen until he heard Fanny.

"Kero..."

Ace instantly pivoted back toward her. Kero had finally answered. Fanny began speaking quickly to the point that her words sounded like a bunch of jumble. Then, with little Josh's cries echoing in the background, he knew that Kero would immediately sense that something was wrong.

As annoying as the dramatic effect was, the thought of it playing on the mental notes of Kero's mind caused Ace to enjoy the symphony of all of Kero's fuck ups.

CHAPTER NINE

Kero

"**S**top teasing me and push that muthafucka *in*," Cookie groaned, placing her feet at Kero's waist. He'd been fucking her for the past hour and some – kind of good but obviously not *good* enough. She'd only caught one nut, while he'd busted three times. She badly needed him to catch her up.

His dick size was decent. It just wasn't standing up to her expectations.

Perspiration heavily protruded from the pores of his flesh as he set his dilated pupils on the beautiful, light skinned ass before him. Cookie was a short, lil, bad thing from around the way, who'd been someone he'd trolled on for weeks until he finally made her an offer she couldn't refuse. And at the moment, she seemed every bit of worth it.

They had popped a few X pills before getting into it, but they hadn't done shit for him. The pussy had already caused him to bust more times than he felt he should have. Usually, when he was geeked, he'd do real damage to a bitch's insides. But whether it was her tight-ass grip or the weak ass X pills, something wasn't letting him last.

Kero ran the head of his dick up and down her slick heat. His jaw tightened as frustration crept its way in. He bit down so hard on his bottom lip that it drew blood. He couldn't bust a fourth time and let her turn him into a laughingstock among her friends.

Nah. That wasn't happening. He had to make this ho respect his dick game.

"You think a nigga bout to keep playing wit yo ass, don't you?" Kero grumbled, dragging a sweaty forearm across his forehead.

Cookie giggled, wiggling her ass tauntingly in front of him. "Oh, that's what you been doin? I thought you was gon tame this pussy… like *you* kept saying. Maybe she *too* much for you."

He exhaled sharply, gripping Cookie's hips, ready to make her eat every last one of those words. Just as he was about to bury himself deep, his phone shook to life, vibrating a little too hard on the nightstand.

Kero clenched his jaw, debating on whether to ignore it or not, but the constant vibrating was killing whatever rhythm he had been trying to vibe to. "Man, what the fuck?" he muttered, snatching the phone up. He pressed it to his ear, irritated. "The fuck going, bra?"

Keith's nonchalant voice came through. "Shawty, they missed the nigga at the tel. He hit, but he did Nut and Chelle…"

"Like hit and still moving?" Kero asked, quickly cutting him off.

"Nigga, the fuck you think if I'm telling you he *did* Nut and Chelle…"

"That's crazy. But…"

"Aye, fuck this phone shit. I need you to pull up asap. We need to look at other options," Keith told him.

Kero began to rub the side of his face as his eyes laid on Cookie. He had come off a nice bit of paper for this moment. And something as simple as answering the phone was about to flush that shit right down the toilet.

"Aye, you got to give me to later on, man. Shit tight right now."

"Nigga, later on? Man, you got a hour to pull up, nigga!" Keith growled through the phone.

Kero gritted his teeth with his free hand turning into a tight fist. Keith was getting beside himself.

"Look, right…" Before he had a chance to get out another word, the sound of the call ending penetrated his ear. He looked at the phone, his lips curling in frustration. Keith had hung up.

Kero inhaled deeply, trying to exhale some tension along with the breath leaving his body. The business deal he had with Keith and his brothers was undeniably a lucrative one, yet sometimes, he wondered if it was actually worth it. Yes, his money had reached a notable level, which was starting to give him access to real power and control. But at what cost?

Too many times had occurred where Keith thought he could talk to – and handle – him any kind of way. Like he was nothing more than a bitch ass worker. At first, he blew it off as just his way of dealing with the grief and all, due to his deceased brother. But now, his disrespect had become too regular. Keith wasn't his boss, wasn't his OG, and definitely wasn't anybody to be throwing orders around like Kero was some fucking runner. Nah, that shit was dead.

His fingers clenched tighter around the phone, jaw clicking. He'd let Keith slide too many times. They needed to have a one-on-one. A real one. Because one thing a nigga like Keith needed to understand was that Kero wasn't anybody's fuckin' flunky.

Before he could dwell on it further, his phone lit up again. *Spain.*

Kero exhaled sharply. *Now what the fuck?*

From the bed, Cookie let out an exasperated sigh. "Damn. You workin or you fuckin? Cuz I don't have all day to be playing."

Kero sucked his teeth, debating whether to ignore it, but deep down, he knew that Spain wouldn't be calling unless it *was* something.

With a heavy sigh, he swiped to answer. "What, Spain?"

"Aye, where you?"

"Nigga, getting some pussy. What the fuck you want?" Kero stepped over to the bed where Cookie turned on her side. He ran his eyes along the length of her physique – from her head down to her pretty ass feet. Then, he heard the sound of another incoming call. *Fanny.* Everybody had him fucked up if they thought he was going to let this pussy pass.

"Bra, you said that bout two hours ago. Nigga, you know we posed to pull up on ol boy bout the safe shit. Then, this nigga, Keith, hit, talking bout a meet. He hit you?"

"Yeah. That shit is nothing though. The nigga just on some more shit because his shit ain't together. We'll get at that fool *later-later.*" Kero's tone was dismissive, but frustration still gnawed at him.

Keith acted like he was the only one running shit, like Kero was some backup muscle instead of a boss in his own right. That wasn't flying any more. He had put in too much work, made too many plays, and had stepped up too many stairs to be treated like a bottom feeder in somebody else's operation.

Niggas like Keith – and Ace – only respected power. And it was about time Keith – along with everybody else – learned that they weren't the only ones in a position of power.

"Well, he made it seem like more than *nothing*. And you already know he gonna start acting like a ho wit all that yelling shit."

"Man, fuck how he feel. Niggas on our time, period. So, again, I'ma catch up wit y'all niggas in a few." Before Spain could respond, Kero hung up. He let out a breath with his head tilting backwards, lifting his face toward the ceiling. He chuckled.

"Girl, I'm bout to fuck the shit outta you." He laughed, more to himself than her.

However, his laughter abruptly ceased. Cookie began to caress the skin of his shaft with her delicate toes. She ran them along the length of his shaft, the softness of her foot sending an erotic sensation through him. Her heel pressed the head of his dick against his thigh while her toes began to toy with his sack.

He slowly exhaled.

But just as fast as the moment came, it left. His phone began to vibrate in his hand.

"No…" Cookie murmured. Keeping the head pinned to his thigh with her heel, she dug her toes deeper into his nut sack.

"Please," he begged, his voice low and desperate.

Then, the phone stopped for a few seconds before it began buzzing again.

What the fuck? Kero's expression became dark. *Keith.* He was more than fed up with constant extra shit. His fist clenched even tighter as more irritation built up inside him. He was more than ready to ignore the call and toss the phone across the damn room.

But when he glanced down at the screen, his frustration momentarily paused. *Fanny.*

His first thought was to set the phone on the nightstand. Yet when he saw the notifications of numerous missed messages – all from his sister – he instantly frowned, knowing that something was definitely wrong. Fanny wasn't the type of person to keep trying, after making the first two attempts, unless something very serious was at hand.

"Fuck your phone then!" Cookie spit out, pushing him a little with her foot after watching him place the phone to his ear.

"Bitch, hol up. This my sister…" It rang twice before his heart skipped a beat. Fanny answered, hysterically crying, with her son – his three-year-old nephew – blaring frantically in the background.

"Fanny, the hell going on?" he asked, immediately sensing that something was very wrong. He couldn't remember the last time he'd heard his sister cry. The sound twisted his stomach into a knot.

"*Fanny?!*" he growled, unable to fully understand her words. Then, his heart skipped another beat upon hearing a male voice in the background before Fanny let out a shriek. A brief rumbling sound came through the speaker.

"Fanny, who the fuck…" Instantly, Kero quickly began dressing while keeping the phone glued to his ear. Right when he was about to stick his left leg in the pants, an angry voice came through the phone. Suddenly, he became stiff as a statue. His heart dropped to the pit of his stomach because this particular voice was unmistakable.

CHAPTER TEN

Ace

"Now, how did we get to this point?" Ace's jawbone clenched instinctively. He hadn't heard this nigga's voice in almost a week.

"A–Ace?" Kero stuttered from the other end of the phone.

"The fuck you think, nigga? Kero, how could you be so stupid? Nigga, you did all that to kill me, and now I'm standing here with your muthafucking sister and nephew…"

"Ace, you got it…"

"Fucking right I got it, lil nigga…" Ace growled, cutting him off. "Shawty, you crossed every line you could think of. Then Sassy…" Ace's words trailed off after the mention of Sassy's name. He looked at Fanny, who'd yelped, placing a hand over her mouth as if a piece of the puzzle had fallen in place.

"As a matter of fact, Kero, how 'bout you tell Fanny how you set me and Sassy up to be killed? Since I set you up." Ace chuckled dryly. "Tell her how you took the bullets out of my gun while I was in the bathroom, you snake muthafucka. And tell her how you did all that, *caused all this*, because you chose to work with the pussy ass Feds."

Ace angrily watched as the realization settled within Fanny's features. Her expression shifted, her lips trembling as the weight of

Ace's words crashed down on her. This was all new to her, something she'd never even considered. And now, she could see it clearly.

Her knees shook as tears relentlessly tumbled down her cheeks. But Ace wasn't done. He still needed her on track.

"Kero, nigga, we came from the same dirt with this shit…"

Kero cut him off. "But we never had the same shit, Ace. You was always the greedy one. Always tryna keep a nigga under you, making sure nobody could ever stand next to you. But me? I'm good on following niggas who ain't tryna put me where they at.

"So, nigga, it is what it is. Take the lil money I got over there. And your safe, it's over there. Take it, just leave Fanny and my nephew out of this. I did what I did, kill me for it."

Ace smiled, biting down on his bottom lip. He was almost impressed – almost.

Kero had stupidly brought his safe here instead of stashing it somewhere secure to be popped. That was sloppy. Real sloppy.

But that was Kero for you, always thinking he was ahead when really, he was right where you wanted him.

"Aight," Ace began to nod his head, "aight. Between us it is, lil nigga. Kero, know that I'm gonna kill you *for real*." He turned his attention to Fanny.

"Are both safes in the same place?" Ace asked her though knowing that nine times out of ten, they were. The apartment was only *so* big.

Fanny bobbed her head. "But I only know the code to one… Kero didn't give me the code for the other."

"Probably because he don't have it. It's mine."

Fanny's eyebrows furrowed. "Why would he bring your safe here?" At this very moment, Fanny wanted to curse Kero's ass out for putting her and her baby in this predicament. And why would he turn on Ace for the *Feds*? Fanny had known her brother to be a lot of things at times, but a snitch was never one of them. None of this was making sense, and she doubted that Ace would do this – and say all that – if it wasn't true.

"That's a good question, which I don't have time to figure out. Take me to them," Ace told her before turning his attention back to the phone.

"How much you got over here, nigga?"

"Bout twenty-eight, man…"

"That a do for now. But I'm still collecting in full, nigga!" he barked before throwing the phone into the wall, bringing a sharp shriek from Fanny.

The loud sound of the device shattering was the only thing which finally caused the three-year-old to settle down. Ace followed Fanny into the back bedroom. He stared at the back of her head, wondering could she sense what he was thinking. Once upon a time, he would have never contemplated ending her beautiful life due to some mischief caused by her brother.

Yet, once upon a time, Sassy hadn't been killed because of her brother's betrayal either.

Back then, Ace had seen them as family. Had felt like they were family. But Kero's actions had shattered every dynamic of that bond, leaving nothing but bitterness in its wake. And true enough, Fanny and her child were innocent in all of this – but so was Sassy.

Ace kept close behind her, blocking out every creeping thought of hesitation. He had come here with two objectives, and nothing – no form of logical justification – was going to keep him from seeing them through.

Kero needed to feel what he had walked around carrying since waking up from his coma.

He needed him to experience the gut-wrenching emptiness that came from losing the person you loved, knowing they were set up to die by someone you considered a brother.

Ace wanted him to reach inside his own chest and feel the same unbearable void – one that belonged to the miserable and lost.

Fanny reached and pulled open the closet door. It was a walk-in, and once she parted the clothing, Fanny dropped to one knee. Nervously, she began punching in the code to Kero's safe.

Simultaneously, the beep and clicking sound penetrated his ears. In that very instant, before Fanny had the chance to glance backwards, Ace set the sight on the side of her head. He closed his eyes, squeezing the trigger.

"I'm sorry, Fanny, rest easy," he mumbled, staring at her a moment before moving her slumped corpse from over his safe; it was next to Kero's. Seeing her lifeless body made him begin to feel some type of way, yet the way he felt had nothing to do with the second objective.

Kero, most likely, was on his way – probably with an entourage. And if he was desperate, he could have possibly called the police. The latter made him clear both safes in no more than a minute and a half. The jewels, money, and a small hand pistol, he stuffed into a baby bag he'd sling over his shoulder.

Stepping back into the living room, Ace immediately noticed that the only sound heard was that of a commercial playing on the television. His retinas quickly fell to the couch where little Josh's small eyes just as quickly found him.

Ace stared into the child's eyes, grateful that he wasn't of the age to understand any of what had taken place. And if he had been, Ace was still pretty sure that he wouldn't have harmed him because adults were one thing, but kids – ever since that night at T-Rock's – remained out of the question, period.

Though hadn't I crossed that particular line with Stacey? he asked himself before he dismissed the thought as collateral damage.

"God bless the child that can hold his own. Revenge will always be yours if I'm still living by the time you realize what happened today, little man." It seemed as if little Josh could sense an interpretation of his words cause, abruptly, he began walking with vengeance lacing the tone of his cries. Ace was about to turn around until he caught a glimpse of something he'd logged in his mental upon entering and something he'd almost forgot about.

A set of keys were on the coffee table, and he knew one of them was the key to the car Kero had gotten her. He'd bought it as a birthday gift. It was small, yet it would do to put some distance between him and Kero's faults.

The sun's rays had just begun dipping below the horizon when Ace pulled away in Fanny's Ford Fiesta S. Once he hit the expressway, he pulled out the burner phone and dialed Ariel.

He laid out everything she needed to know, keeping it short and direct. Then, he told her which train station to meet him at.

He couldn't drive the car forever because there was no telling who was already looking for it. And like most modern vehicles, they were equipped with system trackers, so it wouldn't take much for someone to pull up his location with just a few clicks on a keyboard.

Time was ticking.

Luckily for him, it was after business hours, meaning it would take a serious push from someone high up to get the tracking activated immediately. At least that was what he thought.

Ace hopped off the expressway, rolling to a stop at the busy intersection of Phipps Dr.

The traffic was always thick in Buckhead, which was exactly why he chose it. The Ford Fiesta didn't match the luxury standards of the usual commuters, but that was the beauty of it – nobody would be looking for him here, in this car.

He checked the rearview mirror. Nothing alarming. His gaze shifted to the bright lights of Lenox Mall, a beacon of risk staring him dead in the face. *Too close*. Being in this area days after killing Stacey? Stupid as hell.

But that was the thing. She was dead, and he had gotten away.

Logically, the police wouldn't still be scouring the area for a suspect. They were probably still working the forensics, trying to piece together a case. But searching for the perpetrator? Nah.

They knew – just like he knew – that no criminal would be dumb enough to revisit the scene only days later.

Yet here he was.

Making a left, Ace drove while the thought of Stacey forced its way to the forefront of his mind. Memories from the first time he'd seen her started replaying themselves.

At the time, he believed that she was nothing more than a sexy ass college student he wanted to fuck. Never did he think that a brief introduction and exchange would cause his entire world to crumble before his very eyes.

Nor would he have thought that a five-minute engagement would be the cost of the one life he held dearest in his heart.

Ace's jaw tightened thinking about it. Out of naivety and pure stupidity, he allowed – no, encouraged – something so small to spiral into a full blown atomic bomb.

There was no other way he could – or would – see it. No excuses. No justifications. He had brought Stacey into their lives by chasing a mere moment of satisfaction. This was the sole reason he'd ignored every warning sign.

The first proposition. The card. Then another fucking proposition.

It was as simple as daylight. Stacey was not the person he thought she was. And he had learned that the hard way.

Ace pulled onto a quiet, dark street, parking along the curb. Wasting no time, he speedily began wiping down everything he'd touched.

Being wanted for the murder of a DEA agent was already more than he could chew. But if Fanny's murder got added to the equation?

He wouldn't just be at the top of the most-wanted list. He'd be confirming to the world that he was still in the city, still lurking in the shadows, still tearing shit apart.

And that wasn't part of the plan.

Ace leaned back in the seat for a brief second. Every move he made from this point forward needed to be precise. No more reckless decisions. No more stepping outside of what was already planned. Because one wrong step and he wouldn't be running anymore. He'd be done, game over.

After glancing around a second time, Ace felt comfortable with what he saw – nothing. Stepping out into the night, he threw the baby bag over his shoulder and started his journey toward Brookhaven train station.

CHAPTER ELEVEN

Freshman Black

"Say less. Preciate the heads up, my nigga." Freshman smirked, disconnecting the call. Lonzo had just phoned him, filling him in on what to expect. Tip was sending some niggas to kill him and Hot, which he wasn't too much worried about.

After they'd ran down on Live and Bo – then Mook and the crew – Freshman knew it would only be a matter of time before Hot's spot would be remembered. So, that very same day of Bo's murder, they relocated, finding a three-bedroom townhouse out in Clayton County. However though, Freshman wouldn't miss an opportunity to take advantage of a misdirected opponent.

Which was why he paid a lil female a few thousand to rent out her apartment, which was opposite of the building they'd previously stayed in.

This apartment set at the edge on the third floor. From here, not only could he clearly see the two flights of stairs leading up to the old place, but he could also see the entrance of the complex.

Freshman continued to stare from the side of the curtain. The flow of in and outgoing traffic was sparse, and a hit team the size of what Lonzo mentioned would definitely require a few vehicles if not some noticeable SUVs or vans.

He smirked because little did his ambushers know, they'd be

spotted from less than a mile away. This would easily be the biggest mistake they'd make in their lives.

Turning away from the window, Freshman glanced over at his fellow comrades, two of which were sitting on the couch, lost in their own heads. The other three sat at the small table playing *Pluck*.

He smiled, thinking this was one hell of a stakeout crew. They'd been sitting here for over an hour, waiting for the surprise party they were about to set off with the most perfect set of fireworks.

Using the money they'd taken from Tip's spot, Freshman had tossed a nice chunk Asher's way to secure his interest. Right after that, he paid Ramos a visit. He was the man Swift had recommended after Freshman told him he needed real guns to handle the business. That was when he realized Swift wasn't just a pain in the ass. He was the plug Freshman hadn't expected him to be.

Ramos wasn't just some arms dealer; he was a former military vet, the type who'd spent years in warzones and had brought a whole damn arsenal back with him. His collection was something straight out of a special ops raid – high-powered rifles, suppressed handguns, vests, ammo crates stacked like he was gearing up for a full-scale battle.

Freshman had brought Hot along, a decision he ended up regretting. Hot wouldn't stop asking questions. "How you know this dude? Where the hell he get all this?" Freshman gritted his teeth every time. He hated when people asked too many damn questions, especially when he couldn't give a real answer. He sure as hell wasn't about to tell Hot that a DEA agent had put him onto Ramos or that him and Swift were working both sides of the game.

Freshman checked his watch, shaking off the thought. Time was ticking, and soon, all that military-grade firepower was about to get put to use.

He looked over at Youngin, who bit away at his fingernails. "Say, Youngin…" Freshman said, getting his attention. "You up for the window?"

Youngin nodded his head before even looking at him.

A few days ago, Freshman had met the young dude along with the other three young niggas Hot had recruited for their campaign. Youngin wasn't one of the toughest in the bunch, but you could tell he held his own. He was small like the majority of young niggas these days and thoughtless like them as well. His chosen attire for this affair was a pair of black skinny jeans with a matching Lavish Life T-shirt and a Pokémon cuff beanie cap on his head.

Freshman shook his head to keep the hilarious smile from spreading across his face. He hadn't really paid any attention to any of them since Hot and them met him here. His focus had been on the last text Swift sent him, which he decided to put at the back of his mind until this little matter was handled.

Now that he paid it some mind, Freshman began to gaze over the other three. Lil Joe was on the pudgy side of life with a bronze skin complexion. He was a lil gangsta in his own right, stamping the streets with his presence. He also wore skinny jeans, a pair of retro Nikes, and a fitted hoodie.

Freshman's eyes found the one named Whip. He was short and stocky, wearing basically the same trend as the other two. Then you had the last one of the group, Taliban. He and Lil Joe were the real gangstas of the group. Yet, he was the total opposite of his counterpart.

His frame was a lot slimmer than Joe's, and his demeanor was a lot cooler. When Joe was illogical, Taliban was logical. Where Joe was reckless, Taliban was collective. This made the two a mean duo because you never knew what to expect, Freshman quickly learned.

However, Taliban's attire set him apart from the others as well. He wore a pair of fitted denim jeans, a Seven Continents hoodie, and a pair of Louboutin boots. Truth be told, if the young nigga didn't have the tattoo in the middle of his face and the one trailing the side, he would have thought he belonged to the Morehouse crowd rather than this den of rebels.

Freshman liked the way he moved more than he liked the way his padres did. And if he continued to stay how he was, a ranking spot would definitely have his name on it once Freshman took over the Hand.

Moving about the small living room, Freshman stepped his way over toward the weapons and gear he was ready to put to full use. Leaning up against the wall were four HK 416 assault rifles with fifty-round drums attached and a few thirty-round clips on the floor. There was a Mossberg M500 shotgun. Over from the shotgun were six NIJ tactical, plated vests for every person present.

Hot thought Freshman was crazy when he first mentioned having the vests, but after Freshman explained why they needed them, he fully understood his point. They were going to war with average street niggas, who wouldn't be wearing any form of protective gear at all. Sure, they'd be outnumbered, but the scales would tilt in their favor.

The element of surprise was one thing; the body armor was an edge. Their opponents weren't marksmen either. They'd try to chop them down any kind of way they could – and the bulk of the body would be marked a bullseye.

Thoughts of this war, along with the reminiscent pages of spy novels he'd read throughout those months of *rehabilitation*, caused him to rethink every angle of the way he would go about erasing Tip. He already initiated the *hit-and-run* step by popping up randomly to get a point across. Now, step two was in effect, the *ambush*. Che Guevara said to gradually weaken the enemy, and if this didn't do it physically, it would mentally. He had to show Tip – and everyone else – that he was playing on a higher level in the game.

And thanks to Swift's plug and minor involvement, Freshman was about to do just that.

"Aye," he began, getting everyone's attention, "the nigga say that it'll be some kind of van, a navy-blue SUV, and a carload of niggas headed. It probably a take them bout thirty-forty minutes to get here so go head and piss, shit, do whatever you need to cause when we put this shit on, we ain't doing or thinking about shit until we bury every last one of these niggas. I promised y'all some bread, and you niggas getting the beginning of your wages after this is done. How a forty piece sound?"

They all gave gestures of appreciation, but Lil Joe – as usual – went beyond a simple form of gratitude.

"Man, where these fools at? A forty piece? Nigga, you want they shoes too?" Quickly, he snatched up a vest, sliding an arm through. "This ain't gon take four minutes," he finished, chuckling along with the rest of them.

"Might not even take two, but don't be stupid enough to think that these niggas just a easy walk over. They gon be strapped with more shooters on their side. And they wanna do us just as bad as we want to do them. It's a match made in Heaven." Freshman smirked, staring each one of them in the eyes.

Then his retinas returned to Joe. "When we walk down on them, nigga, we walk all the way the fuck down. We already know the plan. When they go up, we go down and lay til they come back down. We ain't got to do a lot of spreading out. Just spray everything in the hallway. If a few standing guard, we still sticking to the plan."

"Why we don't just be outside waiting for them to pull up then cancel they asses?" Taliban questioned, placing the cards on the table.

Freshman's eyes narrowed as they set on Taliban. He thought about what he said for a second then started nodding his head. "That sounds like the move, but where the hell we gon be standing at out there with all this?" Freshman pointed toward the guns and vests.

"Fresh, we can lay the guns on the ground…" Before Taliban got out another word, Youngin cut him off.

"Ion think we gon make it that far. A van creeping its way through the entrance."

Hurriedly, Freshman moved for the window as everyone jumped to their feet and quickly began suiting up. "Hit the light." He pulled the curtain back a bit. Immediately, he noticed that the van had its headlights off, slowly inching its way forward like it had suddenly cut off. He peered harder; there was a big logo on the side, but he couldn't make it out.

A dead silence fell upon the room. He could hear the distant sound of an ignition revving. Then the van came back to life with its headlights beaming brightly. It didn't turn into the front parking lot like he expected Tip's people to do. Yet the way it crept past shook two alarming bells in his head, encouraging him to further investigate. But there was another lightless vehicle – well, an SUV. It was parked along the curb, a few yards beyond the entrance of the apartments.

It set there like it was watching them, or so he thought. The longer the SUV remained motionless, the more it began to rub him the wrong way. After sliding into a vest, Freshman picked up an HK, racking a round into the chamber. "Watch that fucking truck a few feet away from the gate."

Quickly, he stepped out into the corridor and lightly hugged his way toward the opposite end, then he stole a peek over the rail. The van that stopped was now parked in the middle of the two rows of cars. His eyes mooned. Two men clad in all black were moving directly below him. Taking one step, he peered downward between the railing of the stairs. Freshman saw bits and pieces of bodies making their way up the first flight.

Fuck. Freshman glanced backwards to see Hot. "They coming – catch 'em from that way," he said as loud as a whisper would allow. His attention fell back between the rails. The face of an ambusher was looking up at him. Neither uttered a word. In unison, both, *recklessly*, aimed their barrels and fired. Loudly, gunfire echoed off the hallway's walls. Freshman continued to squeeze the trigger, while Hot and Taliban took a few steps and set their sights on the clique of would-be killers grouped together.

Mercilessly, they fired, sending the group sprawling down the first flight for cover. However, two didn't have a chance. Their bodies instantly turned into shields for their comrades who were hastily trampling over one another as they went down.

Boldly, Taliban relentlessly sent round after round the opps way for every step he took. He wanted to show niggas exactly who they were going against.

Looking over his shoulder, Hot stopped Taliban from taking the last step. "Tali!" he yelled loudly, getting his attention. Hot shook his head and put up a finger for him to wait. He then looked back across the hallway at Freshman inching his way down the stairwell. The complex fell into a deadly silence. It was like the world became still.

Holding his breath, Freshman fired a round into each of the two bodies lying by the second flight of stairs. There wasn't a face peering back up at him this time nor was there any brief movements of shadows. Abruptly, shots began to ring out again. This let him know that those who still chose to fight were determined to hold their ground somewhere below him. Speedily, he leapt over and positioned his back against the wall and eased to the edge of the corridor.

As quickly as possible, Freshman stole micro-second peeks over the railing where he saw the van, a small light pole, and some darkened bushes. After the fourth peek, he realized that the dark patch of what he first thought to be bushes was a lot wider than he remembered them being.

Taking a deep breath, he aimed the muzzle over the rail and squeezed the trigger. Three rounds tore threw the bush before the fourth penetrated a target.

Freshman continued to let loose as he watched the response send sparks from the railing and chip chunks of siding from the complex's walling. However, the angle from which the bullets came told him that one of them was moving…

"Fuck!" Freshman barked. A slug had crashed through the flesh of his hand until slamming into the metal of the HK were it ricocheting its way out the side of the index finger. Snatching the rifle back, his eyes bucked. His elbow had connected with another body behind him. It was Youngin.

"Freshman, come on!" he yelled into his ear. Over Youngin's shoulder, Freshman could see Lil Joe shooting down the stairs close to him. At the opposite end of the corridor, he saw Hot and the others making their way toward the parking lot.

"Come on!" He heard Youngin scream again. For the first time, he looked down at his hand. Blood poured furiously from the torn tissue and ligaments of his left hand.

"Hold this." He pushed the HK to him. "I got to wrap this shit." With one hand, he pulled his shirt over his head and down onto the wound and began twisting it around. Some of his blood being left on the scene couldn't be avoided. But it wasn't all bad. He had an ace in his hand, a man he was sure could not only make a few drops of forensic evidence disappear but could also get him some help without some unwanted attention.

He'd make the call as soon as there was room for him to breathe. "Where your pistol?" Freshman asked Youngin, glancing down at his waist. Keeping the HK wasn't an option, and he refused to be without anything. There were niggas still shooting from the direction of the van, and a few more dudes were at the front of the complex, waiting. They'd need every available hand to help them make it out.

Launching a round into the chamber, Youngin handed the gun to him.

Getting in front of him, Youngin sent a few shots downward and began to move, staying close to Freshman as they went toward the others.

With Joe and Taliban in the front, the six of them descended the last flight of stairs. Lil Joe, being the first one, fired a few shots toward the other end then quickly pivoted around, moving for the entrance of the building where he stopped, peeking out at the parking lot.

The original plan had been for them to catch the would-be ambushers off guard when they came from the old apartment and kill them. After which, they'd load up in the two stolen cars. Both were at opposite ends of the lot where they would have been easy to reach after the slaughter. Now, they'd have to make it to them the best way they could.

Thick beads of sweat began to cover Freshman's face as he leaned up against the wall, waiting for the go ahead. His adrenaline continued to pump yet failed to slow the excruciating pain coming from his hand. Fuck, he didn't need to be left with one hand right now. He came to the realization that soon he wouldn't be doing anything at all if he didn't make it to at least one of the cars and get help to stop the steady flow of blood rushing from his hand.

Fuck, fuck, fuck! His mind instantly began to ramble for the best option available. Too many rounds were fired to not think that the police were on the way. Surely, a resident in the building heard the loud exchange. Once one of them called the law and they heard it in the background, not only were they definitely coming, but they'd be pulling up in numbers. The result would be bad for all parties involved, though Freshman was only concerned with himself getting away.

Aimlessly, he fired three consecutive rounds down the hallway while moving to the wall opposite of his entourage. They couldn't just sit here and keep shooting. "Say, Hot!" he called out. Hot looked over his shoulder. "Aye, you gotta get the car!"

Hot's face immediately wrinkled. "Nigga, you get the car! The hell."

"How?!" Freshman snapped, jerking the blood-soaked cloth upward for him to see.

Hot's brow arched a little. "Soft ass shit."

"Nigga, get the fucking car!" Freshman growled, ready to shoot his ass. He would if he didn't go in the next few seconds because if the police came before they left, they were all dead.

Freshman took a step toward Hot, ready to act, but Taliban cut in first. "I'll go get it," he said.

Before Freshman could react, Hot slapped the keys into the youngin's hand without hesitation.

Freshman's jaw clenched. He wanted to knock Hot's ass out. Him and Hot were the most experienced in the group, and here he was, sending a young nigga to save the day, a kid who had probably never been in a situation like this. Pressure made people do crazy shit, especially when it was their first time in the fire.

But Freshman didn't have time to dwell on it. Right now, all that mattered was getting out of this situation in one piece.

One thing was certain. He wouldn't forget this – Hot's decision nor the inexperience of their soon to be savior. Niggas made their bed. Now, they'd had to lay in it.

Irritated and in tremendous pain, Freshman glanced over the part of the lot he could see. Cars lined both rows, damn near filling each parking space. They'd have to make it over the few steps of the walkway then use the vehicles – one at a time – as temporary shields until they all made it to the whip.

Things hadn't went as planned. Now, Freshman and the crew found themselves in a boxed-in situation where their hopes of making it out of this was to chance getting hit by a bullet or two. But what else was there?

The vehicle of their attackers blocked the entrance of the lot, and the van of the others was in the lot behind, where niggas were still shooting from, at the entrance at the opposite end.

Freshman fired more shots toward the other opening of the building. They couldn't continue to sit right here. "Aye," he yelped, getting their partial attention. "Twelve got to be on the way. We can't keep sitting here. We gots to move."

No one responded.

He peeked at what he could. A light pole set at the edge of the lot. Its rays dimly reached the car where he saw a body leaning over the trunk, obviously trying to get a good shot. The front of the vehicle was a little obscured, yet he caught a spark. Freshman gazed back at the row of cars. He'd have to lead.

Without uttering a word, Freshman dashed from the corridor, shooting. Never in his life had he been so fast. His feet slid over the gravel until his shoulder slammed into the side fender belonging to one of the vehicles he was trying to duck between.

A heavy grunt burst from his mouth. Mistakenly, he'd used his left hand to break his fall. A sharp shriek followed and was quickly swallowed. Bullets began to hit the rear end of the car. He had their attention.

Clenching his jaw, he bit down the crying pain and stumbled his way upward and fired.

Nothing was about to stop him. He dashed and fired his way around five cars before he saw Taliban. He crouched at the rear of the car, lying the HK on the ground.

"What the hell you waiting on?" Freshman smiled, thinking that he was already in the car. This very moment became a depressing one. The clock was ticking.

"No bullets," Taliban barked with an expression that said he was just as depressed.

"Let's do it." Freshman could see the rest of them finally following suit one at a time. They were holding him down, and he'd do the same. Coming up, Freshman shot in the direction of the nigga who'd moved from the opposite trunk and ducked behind another car. The shooting slowed tremendously, letting him know that everyone was close to being bullet-less.

Taliban made it to the driver's door and hopped in. Freshman had squatted behind the car next to it. He'd made his last shot. But Hot and them were across.

It wouldn't take a full minute for them to pack in and pull off.

Taliban pushed the accelerator, sending them rumbling over a curb and onto a section of grass. Passing the second and third lot, Taliban yanked the steering wheel to the left. The car fishtailed, sliding over the moist ground until he snatched the steering wheel again. The vehicle straightened, picking up more speed. Then they all saw the fence…

Forty-two minutes later, Freshman found himself at Wellstar Cobb Medical Center. He texted Swift after Taliban almost killed everyone making their *Fast and Furious* escape. Who would've thought that a fence, a steep ditch, and two barely missed trees would almost cause him to turn his life over to God? Even though he'd woken up in the hospital before after coming close to death, never had he felt the presence of death as Taliban's driving had done.

Miraculously, it freed them from the tight jam they'd unexpectedly found themselves in. Safely, Freshman made it to the hospital. After him and Hot went back-and-forth for more than five minutes, they finally agreed on one thing. They all needed to get the fuck outta that car.

Taliban would drop Hot and the others off near Dixie Hills. Then, as directed by Swift, Freshman told Taliban to let him out a block away from the small medical center he'd pulled up on Google Maps.

The pain of his hand was intensifying, yet it wouldn't prevent him from having tiny thoughts of the obvious. Someone had known where they were camped out in that apartment. How they knew was the question.

CHAPTER TWELVE

Ace

It had taken him nearly twenty minutes to make it to Brookhaven then another fifteen to reach Westlake Station.

Even with the disguise, Ace felt every stare. He kept his head low, but that didn't stop the scrutiny – the way eyes lingered just a second *too* long, shifting between him and the baby bag slung over his shoulder.

Since he was young, Ace hated when people stared. It always made him feel like they had their mind set on him a little too much for comfort. Right now, he felt a lot more than uncomfortable.

After what felt like an eternity of torture, Ace finally reached Westlake Station and stepped off the train. He had called Ariel just before hopping off, ensuring she'd be waiting for him in the parking lot.

Keeping his strides long and deliberate – but not too urgent and not enough to draw suspicion – he scanned the lot, locking onto the car within seconds.

Without hesitation, he reached the vehicle, yanked the door open, and slid inside, dropping the baby bag onto the floor.

Before he could shut the door, Ariel quickly tugged him to her and began kissing him like she hadn't seen him in years. Her tongue tasted so good to him that he was trying to remember what the tongue between her legs tasted like. *Damn!* Ace had to force himself to pull his lips free of hers.

The corner of his mouth inched upward. "That's how you feel?"

Ariel bit down on her lower lip, her eyes dropping to the crotch of his jeans before locking back onto his.

"I need to feel you inside me one more time before I leave." Her hand slid down, fingers pressing into the thick outline beneath the denim, squeezing just enough to send a pulse of heat through him.

Ace exhaled sharply, glancing around. "You think that's a good idea? With all this anti-sweat shit on my face?"

They were still in the parking lot of the train station where a few light poles stood scattered, casting faint glows over the area.

The last thing he needed was to end up on MARTA police's radar over some reckless shit.

"Then right here?" he asked, raising an eyebrow, feeling his control slipping already.

"Who said you was doing anything? And I don't think anyone's gonna be a problem."

Ariel smirked, pulling the pistol from under her thigh and slid it onto the dashboard. At the same time, her other hand slipped into his pants, fingers wrapping around him with slow and deliberate pressure.

"You… serious?" Ace exhaled again, his breath hitching as the warmth of her palm massaged his length, coaxing him to full hardness.

Reflexively, the floor of his pelvic muscle tightened, blood rushed through his veins, thickening him into a solid structure. "A…" He wanted to protest, but she cut him off before he could get the words out.

"I got this. Now, let your seat back and pull these down some," Ariel demanded, tugging at his waistband with a firm grip.

Ace exhaled a third time, following instructions as her fingers tightened around him, sending a pulse of heat through his core.

She reached over, turning the volume up as Summer Walker's *Girls Need Love* flowed through the speakers. The sultry melody filled the car, blending with the heavy tension riding the air.

Ariel pressed her nose against his cheek, her breath warm, teasing the edge of his lips. She shifted, maneuvering herself onto one knee in the driver's seat, her body igniting with fire.

Her free hand disappeared beneath the hem of her dress, gliding upward to part the softness between her thighs.

A deep, fiery flow of ecstasy radiated from her core, a sensation that started as a whisper before rolling through her body in waves. The swollen lips of her pussy tingled, salivating at the mere anticipation of what was to come.

A sexy moan escaped her mouth as her fingers found the slick crevice and slipped inside.

Ace felt a new rush of blood push through more than just one body part. For the first time in his life, he questioned whether getting some pussy was worth the risk. Too many times before, he had thought so – but back then, his life hadn't been on the line.

His gaze locked onto Ariel's darkened pupils, the weight of another dangerous decision settling in his mind. He was about to take a risk that he knew he shouldn't – *but fuck it.*

Ariel leaned in, kissing him with slow passion before withdrawing her hand from his stiff length. Her smirk glowed faintly in the dim light as her fingers traced down his lower abs.

Then, her head dipped toward his lap.

She pushed saliva to the very tip of her tongue, letting it ease off in a warm stream onto the swollen head of him. Her lips parted, quickly chasing the glistening spit, catching up to it after she'd took in enough inches to fill her small mouth.

Ace groaned as her tongue swirled, her throat instinctively tightening around him. The thrust made her gag slightly, sending an unintended rush of lubrication down his shaft.

She needed one last taste of him before their time together slipped away into an uncertain future.

Ace had been on her mind since she dropped him off earlier. For hours, Ariel had replayed every moment they'd shared, every instant they'd created and forged into something unforgettable. At the time, she badly wanted to drop a tear for each minute they'd miss after today.

Then, something clicked. She couldn't change the future, but she could take something with her to remember.

Ariel twisted her succulent mouth free from his manhood, a knowing smile spreading across her lips.

The same two fingers she had buried inside herself, she now slid between Ace's lips, letting him taste her while she positioned herself over him.

With one foot braced against the door rest, she squatted over him, teasingly rubbing his moist dick against her clit.

Then – slowly – she guided him inside her dripping love.

She gasped, her insides clamping around his shaft as she rocked her way down him.

"Fuck..." she moaned, wanting to feel every inch, every deep stroke. Ariel rotated her hips, tightening her grip around him as she began to ride with slow, thoughtful strokes before picking up speed. Her hand clutched onto his shirt, the other gripping his neck, barely missing the fake beard.

I want it, her mind screamed as she threw herself back-and-forth on him, taking him deeper with every thrust.

Ace quivered, his breath hot against her lips as he pulled her face closer.

"Beat that shit harder," he coached, sliding a hand to her ass to help drive the collision.

Their bodies moved in sync, skin slapping in rhythm, the wet sounds of their connection filling the car like an African drumbeat.

Ariel's moans turned into desperate whimpers as she rode him relentlessly, the heat between them unbearable. Her walls squeezed, milking him as her climax ripped through her.

Ace groaned, his grip tightening as his own release followed, his body jerking beneath her as he emptied himself deep inside.

Their breathing was ragged, their hearts were exhausted, and their bodies remained locked in the aftermath of their dance.

After a few seconds of stillness, Ariel slowly lifted herself off him, her legs trembling. Without a word, she reached for the small towel on the backseat and quickly cleaning them both before climbing back into the driver's seat.

Ace sat back and watched as she straightened her dress and smirked.

She exhaled, gripping the wheel. "That definitely was a goodbye present."

Ace chuckled, adjusting himself in his seat. "Shid…"

Without another word, Ariel started the car and pulled off. The weight of reality settled back in both of their minds as the city lights blurred past them.

As they rode, Ace counted and gave Ariel forty of the seventy-one thousand. Then, he got one last look at the jewelry before placing it into her purse.

Ace couldn't believe the safe had remained in the condition he'd last seen it in. He guessed Kero hadn't thought that far ahead by having someone already on hand to bust it. And Ace was grateful he didn't. The twenty-eight, plus the forty-three thousand he collected from his safe, would surely be enough to hold both of them down. Well, until he found the *real* jewels, which he didn't have a *real* plan for locating at the moment.

Stacey had given him the area Greedy Spence frequented but not an address. She'd mentioned something about a man named Eric Swift, who possessed the actual address and didn't trust her enough to relate it. And he, she also said, was the same muthafucka who orchestrated Sassy's kidnapping.

Ace would never forget the name Eric Swift, nor would he forget the face it belonged to. The photo online had been taken a few years ago, he realized after noticing the small, printed date at the bottom, but how much could the man have changed? Ace hoped not much because…

He shook his head before the thought dragged him to a place he did not want to be. Eric Swift had a day somewhere on his mental calendar and becoming a little too overly focused on all the things he wanted to do to him would not bring it any closer than he already was. *But when it do finally come…*

Ace looked over at Ariel and stared a moment. The outline of her soft skin made him want to just pull her close and snuggle his face up against hers. His eyes trailed down her body until settling on her impregnated tummy. There brewed another life which he helped procreate into existence.

At this very moment, Ace could honestly admit that he wanted the world to see another part of him just as bad as the world wanted to see it. What else could explain it?

Out of all the females he'd sexed without condoms, only the two who held his heart had carried his seed. It was like destiny was determined to throw a true symbol of his love out into the sea of creation. And at this point, he wanted nothing less than that. He wanted to leave the world a piece of him to be remembered by.

"What?" Ariel asked, finally acknowledging his stare.

"I want my story to always be remembered," he said, fixing his gaze on the night's sky.

"It will, baby."

"No, for real. I want my story written so that our child's children can understand that they're sacrifices that have to be made for the lives of the ones you love." Ace rubbed her stomach, causing the corners of her mouth to crease upward.

"I remember one day, me and White were going somewhere, and bra just kept going on and on about faith. He said, long as I kept faith in the Quran, everything would work out exactly how it was meant to *inshallah*." Ace chuckled after mentioning the Arabic word Whiteboy occasionally uttered. "If we have a boy, I want you to name him Quran because he is what I'm putting my faith in."

"And what if it's a girl? Then?" Ariel questioned.

"Name her Queen…"

Ariel's heart skipped a beat at the mention of the name. She remembered telling him about her older sister, yet she was certain that she never uttered her name to anyone in Georgia. And that would not be the name of any child she brought onto this earth.

"We'll think of something else for a girl name," she said after her mind entertained a brief memory of the past. She'd never forget the love she'd lost due to the selfish ambitions of her sister. Ariel didn't want to think about her. She'd have time for that once she made it home.

Ace caught the vibe instantly. The sudden change in her tone of voice let him know that there laid something behind the rebuke of that particular word. However, their time was short, and he refused to waste a minute of it on a thing she obviously wasn't comfortable with. "So, how long do you think it'll take you to reach Virginia?"

"Shouldn't take no more than bout seven long hours of boring driving. My family in Richmond."

"When the last time you saw them?" Ace asked. He remembered bits and pieces of her story because she never flat out told it. Ariel made it clear that whatever she had left in Virginia stayed in Virginia.

She gave a halfhearted laugh. "It's been what – close to four or five years. It's gonna be crazy just popping back up – and pregnant." Ariel couldn't wait to see all the cheerful, shocked, and dismissive expressions from the people she'd left. Then, there were the evil daggers that would come from her older sibling, which she'd definitely return. She couldn't wait.

"I already know it is. What you think they gonna say?"

"Ain't no telling with them crazy ass people. But all that's for when I get there. You sure about this Trigga guy helping you?"

"I'm really not sure about anything…" Ace truthfully said. "White was the mutual person between us, and he fucked with Whiteboy hard. And to top it off, he already got some beef shit going on with the Italians. I don't see why he wouldn't. When I tell him they killed White…"

Ariel looked over at Ace for a second. She was debating with herself on whether or not to mouth what she'd been thinking about when he was dealing with Kero's sister. Giving him false hope was not what she intended, but there was something that was not making sense.

"Bae, about Whiteboy. I been hearing *both* of y'all names all over the radio still. Don't you think…"

"Don't," Ace muttered, cutting her off before she took him back down the road he'd been down a thousand times since leaving the officer in the middle of the street. "White is dead."

"But…"

"But what? A, I seen him on the stretcher with my own eyes," Ace growled. He didn't mean for his tone to be so aggressive. That was a sensitive area for him to touch right now. When he had woken up in the hospital, people had told him that Sassy died. It had taken months for him to come to grips with the reality that the love of his life was no longer a part of this world.

Too many days he'd wasted on trying to construct a day when he'd wake up and realize that it was all just a bad dream – that she was patiently waiting for him to reunite their souls. Ace lost himself by not dealing with what *was*. And Whiteboy *was* dead.

Ariel twisted her lips. "You seen *somebody* on the stretcher, Ace. You don't think, as deep as this shit is, that -by now, it would of been broadcasted to the world that one of the niggas they saying killed a federal agent was shot to death?"

Ace didn't respond. Earlier, he'd thought the same. Though as well, he knew how the system – as a collective – fucked up at times, and this was probably one of those times.

However, Whiteboy – unlike Ace – had been arrested and sent to prison. Both institutions collected more than enough information to identify an individual. Why they hadn't figured out who he was by now was not his job to sort out.

"I'ma call you when I reach the nigga, so you'll know what I got going on. If I don't hit you, then…" His words trailed off. The only reason he wouldn't call was the worst-case scenario. He refused to let his last words to her be him speaking ill on himself.

They were now turning off Edgewood Avenue, leaving him with only a few seconds to utilize before necessity pulled them apart for God knows how long.

"You gonna *hit* me until you make it back to me," Ariel told him. She didn't see it any other way.

"I love you – and you," Ace said, rubbing her stomach.

"We love you, Ace." Ariel brought the vehicle to a stop. She pulled him to her by the chin and pressed her lips against his for the last time. She was going to miss him.

Ace stepped out. Their eyes locked onto each other before he shut the door. Standing in the night, he waited until the car had vanished into the darkness. He then stared down Mason Avenue. For some odd reason, it felt like he was stepping out of Missy's house all over again, facing the world – alone – again. Again looking to a stranger for help. The only difference between then and now was that then he was an innocent child, afraid of the world. Now, he was an animal for the world to be afraid of.

CHAPTER THIRTEEN

Ace

Ace treaded over the shattered concrete, which had once been a full sidewalk. Now, patches of weeds and roots were covering a good portion of it. He looked around, knowing the hood all too well and exactly how to reach the house Trigga had taken them to after they'd pulled the lil jewelry heist.

Getting to it wasn't what he was worried about. Whether Trigga was there or not was what had him. He couldn't think of any nigga that willingly stayed in a place he'd set up to be everything besides a home. However, he also knew if Trigga wasn't present, one of his minions would be.

Keeping his gait unsuspicious, Ace trekked his way through a few short cuts until he came out on Laura Street. Shockingly, the street was vacant, which was unusual for this dead-end. At a distance, he could see the house. The lights told him that someone was there, and he was about to find out who exactly they were.

Impatiently, Ace headed in its direction. Every few steps he took, Ace stole a look around as if he was anticipating something unexpected to occur. This was a hood where anything could happen.

The house was over thirty feet away. Ace slowed, turning his walk into a stagger. He moved like he belonged – another lost soul treading aimlessly to meet some fate.

The street was so quiet that the sound of a lock clicking almost caused him to stop. Slowly, he gazed around, thinking the sound had come from one of the houses across the street. But nothing moved.

A man laughed as the door came open. Ace's attention snapped toward the laughter's direction. His pulse quickened. Someone had come out of Trigga's spot. The dim porch light flickered as the man skipped down the stairs. The front door remained opened. Another person walked out, shutting the door behind him.

Damn. He wondered how far he could push his luck before it ran out. Ace wasn't sure; he only hoped it didn't run out right now.

The first guy had reached the back of the vehicle in the driveway with the second guy following suit a few feet behind.

"Nigga, you got life fucked," the second guy said loud enough for the entire street to hear.

"Bro, you the one that said you like to put ya legs on hoes' shoulders and wrap 'em round they head while you getting served up," the first man returned while staring down into his phone. "I'm just saying… what if one of those times you do that shit and the ho drop some spit in ya ass, like she tryna clean that muthafucka?" He laughed, bending over on the trunk of the car.

"I promise you I'ma punch that ho ass out. On God!" The second guy noticed the bum heading toward them for the first time. His eyes narrowed suspiciously. *The fuck Unk got going on?*

"What's up?" he asked, causing the first guy to put his attention on the sluggardly approaching person.

Ace didn't say anything. He needed them to think he was a little discombobulated. Once they let their guard down, he'd make a move he doubted they'd be prepared for.

"Say, Dad, the hell you got going on?" The first guy glanced around, realizing that no one else was out here besides them.

Making his voice sound cracked and vexed, Ace begged for change. "Youngblood, y'all," he coughed, "y'all got some change or anything I can get some'n to eat with?" Continuing to stumble forward, Ace stretched his hand out some, as if they were digging into their pockets. But they weren't.

"Aye, Unk, get the fuck on somewhere. Ain't nothing going on."

Stuffing the phone down into his pocket, the first guy took a step toward him. The second one seemed to be unbothered and unthreatened.

"Please, man… I'm hurting bad out here, man. Anything a help…" Ace hunched his shoulders and slightly crouched over with an arm across his stomach.

"What the fuck I just say?" the guy snapped aggressively. He took the last step between them and roughly shoved Ace backwards though not hard enough to make him fall.

Stumbling, Ace cowered back a little, lifting a shaking hand harmlessly. "Blood, all I'm trying to do is put some'n in my stomach, baby. Damn." Ace inched his way in the guy's direction again. Patience was the key.

"Nigga, Ion give a fuck! I just told yo ass ain't shit for you over here. Don't fuck around and make me beat yo ass out here!"

Turning a bit to the right, Ace braced himself for the push. The arm dropped from his stomach, down toward his waist. Roughly, the man latched onto Ace's coat. Timing the jerk and the forward shove perfectly, Ace went along with the motion then reacted in a split second.

Using a foot, Ace instantly halted his movement and pivoted into the guy with more strength than he expected. Before the guy knew it, he was sent backwards into the trunk of the car by his throat.

"The fuck." The second guy took a step back, reaching for his strap, but he was too late. Ace already had the 3D suppressor kissing the man's cheek.

"Nigga, pull that shit and I'ma blow half this nigga's face off," Ace growled menacingly yet not loud enough to alert anyone else who might have been inside the residence.

Dumbly, the second man paused like he'd become frozen. Ace wanted to laugh. It was evident that this new generation had no sense at all. Not only had they both allowed someone unknown to walk up on them, but the second guy had now blown all their chances of surviving this out the window for both of them – if he had intended on killing them. He guess luck was on their side as well because he wasn't there to bring them harm. But they didn't know that.

"Unkkkk… hol on…" Shock and a tad of fright quickly replaced the tough-ass demeanor the captured initially approached him with. Fucked up positions had a way of doing that.

"Nigga, shut the fuck up and turn around." Ace pressed the suppressor against his patch of dreads, then he looked back over at the statute in the yard. "Ease ya strap out and let it hang by a finger. But first, put a hand behind your head."

Ace rapidly switched his eyes between the two until the man extended the pistol toward him – by a finger.

"Place it on the roof – and soon as you do, nigga, you better run yo ass up the street like the Red Dogs behind you, or shawty right here won't see tomorrow – and you neither."

Nervously, the guy did as instructed and wasted no time in sprinting away from them.

*I guess he got a lil sens*e, Ace thought after watching how fast he was moving.

"Young, stupid ass nigga out here playing gangsta when he could of used them legs on somebody's field," Ace said to no one in general. His undivided action was back on his lonely hostage. He eased off him a little, taking a step back. Even the barrel had put a few inches between it and the captured cranium.

"And yo tough ass…" Ace snarled. Noticing the bulge in his pocket, he ripped the gun away. "Now, slowly grab that other one."

Ace stopped him. He was going in the wrong direction. "Nigga, lean cross and grab it." After Ace secured both pistols, he told him to pull out his phone and call Trigga.

"Trigga?" the guy asked, dumbfounded, pausing with the phone in his hand.

"Nigga, call Trigga or make peace with God." Ace pushed his hand forward with the gun until his arm had fully extended. The guy unlocked his phone and proceeded in calling. Sweeping his retinas over the scenery, nothing moved as far as he could tell. Though there was still a chance that the runner doubled back and was somewhere close, watching. Foolishly, Ace hadn't thought to take the man's phone before he took off. He should have.

He heard the distant sound of the phone ringing as his mind began to turn over the possibility of the runner calling reinforcements, his only possible reaction. *Fuck.* Ace needed to get moving fast and not the street way unless he wanted to come across the wrong carload of nig…

"Bra, it's a nigga…" He didn't get to finish delivering the unfolding news. Ace snatched the phone away

"Get the fuck on!" Ace pushed him toward the direction his homie ran in.

"Trigga?" he asked, stepping with newfound purpose.

"Who the fuck is this?" Trigga angrily questioned. It sounded like his blood was on a high boil and rising.

Ace became partly surprised that the calm, in control, and collected *Trigga man's* attitude was anything but that. Finally, Ace had found a way to unsettle his calm waters.

"Don't say my name. This the nigga the *white* boy introduced you to." Ace came to a brief stop at the corner of the house. His eyes quickly analyzed the cut he'd be taking for any signs of life. He then continued on.

"What the fu…" Trigga sounded like he'd run out of breath. This let Ace know that he'd also caught wind of the latest breaking news.

"Yeah, shit crazy. But I need ya help." Ace didn't have time for a conversation. Trekking through the dark, wooded pathway, Ace tucked away his pistol and fished out the burner phone. While Trigga continued to talk, he took the phone from his ear and quickly keyed Trigga's number into the burner. The iPhone he'd confiscated – like all iPhones – had the ability to ping its location to another iPhone in seconds. Getting rid of it before it became a fatal option was his only option.

"You said you need my help?" He heard Trigga say upon pressing the phone back against his ear. "Boy, you need more than help. You need prayer, which I don't have a lot of…"

"Shawty, they set us up and killed Whiteboy." For the first time since he'd walked off with ol boy's phone, he stopped. The words sounded surreal coming out of his mouth. They caused him to stare off aimlessly into the darkness for a moment. After taking a very deep breath, he started to walk again.

"Killed Whiteboy? Nigga, you serious?" It didn't take long for Ace to pick up on the concern riding his voice. It sounded genuine.

"Dead serious."

"Who?"

"Look, I'ma hit you from another number. Pick up – and call off your troops." Ending the call, Ace turned, throwing the phone toward the pitch black from which he came. Crossing a street, he began jogging through another wooded pathway.

He was in a hurry to get as far away from this vicinity though not because of Trigga's lil *do* boys. Missy's house set a few streets over. Ace had taken the biggest risk of tonight by coming over here. Everyone knew the second place the police always searched was the place the person considered home. They would make their presence and overall mission more than known.

And now that he thought about it, he hadn't seen one police cruiser nor anything that said POLICE. He wanted it to stay like that.

Maneuvering through cut after cut, Ace finally made it to the trail that ran from Edgewood to Kirkwood. Placing hands on his knees, he caught some of his breath while peering around at the largest opening within the midst of the woods – an opening he considered as the perfect safe zone regardless the time of day. Ace couldn't remember one time when he'd seen more than two or three people on it at a time.

He phoned Trigga, letting him know where he was. He told Ace to stay put until he got there.

CHAPTER FOURTEEN

Ace

Ace took a seat on the metal railing coursing the trail, thinking about what his next play should be. He didn't know how far Trigga's generosity would go, and he'd be a super fool not to conjure up a few contingency plans. *But what could be actually planned?* he asked himself.

Being a very sought out fugitive really didn't allow plans to be made and followed. Every second on the run brought with it unintended and unexpected – unplanned – occurrences no person could foresee. Fortunately for him, each unthought of event had worked in his favor. Being appreciative was an understatement in describing the way he felt about it. So far, luck had stuck its hand in each situation and had fingerfucked every risk. It seemed as if life finally came to the conclusion that he'd been dished enough fucked up predicaments – and way too many calamities.

How long will this luck last? he asked himself realistically, aware nothing lasted forever. Yet should that have prevented him from still wanting to know?

The answer avoided him. Either way, he'd continue to be thankful for what he could and calculating for what he couldn't.

Ace's head snapped to the left upon hearing what he thought

sounded like a tree branch being trampled over. He smoothly pulled the pistol from his pocket and listened carefully for another crunch.

It never came. Close to an hour passed before the burner vibrated to life. It was Trigga finally.

"Yeah…" he answered, coming to his feet. His ass became numb from the hard railing. Ace didn't even know that the blood circulation to his buttocks was capable of being cut off.

"Where you?"

"Same spot. You close?"

"Hell yeah, bout to pull up now."

As soon as he said it, Ace saw a pair of headlights turn at the end of the street. Instantly, he began moving toward the car cautiously. Anything was still very possible, and he refused to let that fact escape his mind.

"Nigga, what the hell?" Trigga muttered after Ace hopped in.

"Had to switch it up. My face a hot topic," Ace replied, relaxing his grip on the pistol.

"I know that's right. Shawty, how in the hell y'all get caught up in the murder of a Fed? And Whiteboy?" Trigga questioned seriously, pulling away.

"They killed my baby mama and tried to kill me," Ace let out flatly. There was nothing to lie about at this point. The entire truth would be out before long. He was going to make sure of it if he wasn't allowed a chance to experience a piece of his unborn's life.

Trigga raised an eyebrow. "Talking bout…"

Ace nodded his head.

"Damn."

By the way Trigga looked at him, he knew it was all beginning to register. That fateful night in Cobb had been put on display for the world then suddenly snatched from the media and covered up by the people who'd suffer the most damage had a little more light been shed on the situation.

Agents of the federal government were implicated in murder, kidnapping, drugs, and all sorts of other shit. Despite those allegations, he was told to stick to his street code – no snitching – and the government's deepest condolences came with a warning – keep quiet about what happened in Cobb until an *internal investigation* was complete. And if he wanted to avoid getting slammed for murder, drugs, and all sorts of other shit, he'd do exactly that.

At the time, Ace was too lost in grief to even think about speaking, period. His mind was consumed by memories of a time gone, and when it wasn't, Stacey's face was there. He cared less about investigations or any of those fake ass prison threats because the damage was done. He was broken with nothing else to break.

Sassy had died. His choices had sealed her fate. How many times could he say sorry? How many times should he have begged harder for their places to be switched?

Ace found himself drowning in a sea of sorrow and regret. His life became reduced to agony and self-pity, longing for a day when his tormented soul ceased to exist.

But the universe had other plans. Death ignored him. Sassy rejected the pleas of what he desired. Then he woke up.

Life's face had waited for him – and so had the faces of those involved. He needed to prepare, though for what? Black was dead, Stacey was a Fed, and Uncle Sam told him to shut the fuck up.

He did because revenge seemed like the rest of the story – a thing to ponder but having no part of the reality written by the narrator.

However, the story wasn't close to being finished. Ace lived and so did the undiscovered elements of the narration.

"I know I caught you off guard with this shit. And trust me, if I felt like I had another option, I would of taken it. But there ain't none. You the only person I can think of that know some'n bout them mafia muthafuckas…"

Trigga raised a curious eyebrow. "Mafia?"

Ace nodded his head again. "Yeah, the nigga, Paul, set us up…" From there, Ace related everything he thought necessary to convince him. He didn't sugarcoat anything because there was nothing to hide if he was going to die at the end of it all.

Trigga seemed to be listening. Ace needed him to see that he'd lost everything, and if Trigga couldn't help him, then he was on his own.

Desperation leaked from his words, but fuck it, this wasn't the time to be prideful.

Ace didn't realize how long he'd talked until Trigga pulled the vehicle up an off ramp. He glanced around partly then peered up at the dimly lit sign which read, Sigman Rd. Ace had never heard of it.

"Ace," Trigga began, "that's some wild ass shit right there. I really can't even understand it. But you said them agents took some diamonds, and then, one of them ran off with them?" Months and months ago, Trigga heard a story about the thievery of some jewels. But DEA agents being the thieves and executors of a particular son never reached his ears. That was too big of a revelation. He needed to fish more.

"Yeah, that's what ol girl said. Spence Costello is the one on the other side of the country waiting for his moment to enjoy the American dream." Ace recalled what Stacey said about why Spence hadn't dumped the stones.

"Ace, I promise he still has them. He can't just outright sell then. Those stones have laser-inscribed serial numbers. Trying to get rid of them any kind of way would be a big mistake. The old man has more connections than a spider web."

"But y'all took them." Ace thought of how funny it was that she figured telling him all this shit of no concern had a chance of saving her life.

"Yes. Because we have a high-end fence who has guaranteed to bring nothing less than eighty percent of what they're worth."

"And that's supposed to do what for me?" Ace was only prolonging to make sure she felt what Sassy had waiting on death. He wanted her to see each passing second as a sign of hope, which Sassy most likely did.

"Everything, Ace. Take the money and buy you a future…"

"A future." Ace chuckled, amused. *"I don't have a high-end fencer."*

"I do. I'll give you everything. I promise…"

That, along with a few other parts of their conversation, Ace hadn't said to anyone besides himself over and over…

Trigga made a left under the traffic light. "You believe what she said about the *diamonds*?"

"Paul believed her," Ace said, thinking about the expression Paul displayed after realizing he'd stumbled across too much information.

"Paul." The name left Trigga's lips mistakenly.

Ace studied him. "Let me ask you some…"

"After I ask you this." Trigga cut him off. Something was itching the back of his brain. "You said Paul reached out to y'all after the lil jewelry shit. Not to kill y'all but to use you to put some work in on a Fed that been crossed you. Then he fucked over you? Sounds familiar, but I'm just confused about you and Whiteboy pulling up on *Paul* after y'all seen how wicked shit was to get in the mall. Was he asking about me?"

Abruptly, Trigga pulled the car over to the shoulder of the road. Ace's fingers slid back around the handle of the gun. The quick pull over made the vibe clear. There was a faint glint of metal. Ace now noticed how late he was. Trigga's gun found a target.

Ace stared him in the eyes. "Nigga, why the fuck would he be asking about you? And you having beef with a nigga don't dictate the way I plant my fucking feet, nigga!"

Trigga smirked, keeping the gun where it was. "It's odd that his brother saw us together – who I'm betting was the same pudgy fuck that you said pulled up on White. But Ion see him keeping our *acquaintance* from Paul. And I definitely can't see Paul failing to acknowledge it."

Ace kept silent a moment. Trigga seemed ready to lay his hand out on the table. "He did mention you," he began, looking away from him for a brief second. "Told me to stay the fuck away from you because you bad for business, and," Ace wished he had a drumroll to compliment the message, "you're bad for living. He made it clear you bout to die."

Trigga smiled. "That's some ironic shit… Here I was thinking that *y'all* had been trading information." He placed the pistol on his lap and put the car in gear.

"So much for your thinking – but since we on the subject, how bout you tell me something?" Ace continued to slide the gun – unnoticeably – from the coat's pocket. A slip was a slip. "How you know Paul?"

By the time Trigga was done with his story, they were pulling into the driveway of a two floor, brick home. The property set back a good distance away from the road. Ace had paid close attention and attempted to memorize each turn they'd made since getting off the expressway. Yet he'd done it in vain because at this very moment, he couldn't recall anything more than going back down the street and making a left. Beyond that was anybody's guess.

The security lights illuminated the slab of concrete they'd parked on. Ace noticed there were a few lights on inside the residence.

"It's crazy how life be playing out. Sometimes you just got to let life be life…" Trigga was saying as he grabbed a few items off the backseat.

"Life outta control," Ace returned, really not understanding what he meant. Life was life, and it would continue to be life whether a person thought they were letting life be or not. He was a living testament of that because his life was not what he wanted it to be nor what he ever imagined it being. He had no hand in its construction, only two feet to walk it.

"It definitely is. Let's do it. Shid, you gonna be good out here. Nobody comes out here unless I bring them. You can say it's my lil *leave the world behind* resort." He chuckled then stepped out.

Trigga did him a big favor by bringing him somewhere he could likely rest at. Yet that was still to be proven, which was why Ace kept his fingers around the gun. His life was on the line, no matter where he went, and even though Trigga seemed to be genuine with his help, Ace wasn't going to be relaxed enough to believe all was well. It would never be.

"Nigga, I wish I could leave the world behind," Ace muttered as he followed Trigga under the beaming lights and into the two-car garage. He glanced around, taking in the setup as they moved into the main part of the house.

Ace had to admit that he was impressed. When Trigga called this place a little getaway, he hadn't expected it to look like a cross between a library and an art museum. From the garage, up the stairs, and into the hallway, paintings of Black art lined the walls, giving the place an Afrocentric vibe.

By the time they reached the kitchen and stepped into the living room, Ace could tell Trigga was an avid reader. Stacks of books covered nearly every surface. They were piled up on the counter, the couch, the coffee table, and even the floor, like Trigga had been cramming in information for an exam.

Ace couldn't think of one street nigga he'd ever seen with even a single book, let alone this many. Hell, there were so many that he didn't even notice the absence of a TV, stereo, or game system – just books, a few basic furniture pieces, and more books.

Maybe that was why Trigga always acted like he knew everything. Hell, after running through all these, he probably did.

"A nigga can never do too much reading," Trigga muttered, catching Ace's surprised expression before he disappeared down the hallway.

"Shid..." Ace chuckled softly, his mind already feeling overwhelmed by the sheer volume of books. He slid onto a stool, running his fingers across the spines. *Revolutionary Suicide*, *Taste of Power*, *Blood In My Eye*, and *To Die for the People* caught his attention. Ace didn't know much about these books, but he recognized Huey P. Newton's name from his leadership of the Black Panthers. His eyes wandered to the nearby stack, all Black literature. One book in particular grabbed his focus – it was titled *Die Nigger Die* by H. Rap Brown. He opened it, the first few lines immediately drawing him in with their sharp intensity.

As Ace read, the words stirred something in him – an unshakable feeling that he was in the presence of something much larger than street life. These weren't just books; they were echoes of struggles, movements, and mindsets. The more he read, the more a weight settled on his chest, as though every page was challenging him to see the world differently.

"You grow up in Black America and it's like living in a pressure cooker. Babies become men without going through childhood. And when you become a man, you got nothing to look forward to and nothing to look back on. So what do you make it on?"

Ace stopped, rereading those lines over. How did that small section of words basically explain his life? He was a product of Black America with no childhood, and what was there for him to look forward to? How had this H. Rap Brown guy been so accurate?

He sat there a moment, giving it some thought. Here was someone he'd never heard of laying out a perspective of his reality from which he hadn't recognized as a point of view. That went beyond the scope of his existence. Brown had used his words as a general appliance regarding the Black experience in America.

No Black person on this land had to be told that, by their color alone, they were automatically subjected to the discriminate disadvantages imposed by the European society as a whole. You didn't have to go to school to learn that your people were always at the bottom of someone's totem pole. The commonality of this realization had been set in stone before his time, and still today, its theme played on the mental notes of Black conscious – unconsciously.

"Nigga, what you know about Al-Amin?" Trigga asked, coming back into the kitchen.

"Who?" Ace questioned, gazing over another page.

"The man who book you reading," Trigga told him incredulously, pulling open the frig. "Aye, you want some'n to drink? I don't drink a lot of shit, so it's three choices – water, apple juice, and milk?"

"Water a do." Ace gazed over the book's cover. The concept of the picture caused his brows to furrow. There was a Black man, apparently cuffed, displaying an expressive mixture of pain, confusion – and helplessness as four white police officers subdued him in a manner Black males were all too familiar with.

The old, black and white photograph looked as if it was taken in the sixties or seventies. Ace wasn't sure, though he was about one thing: the narrative of Black repression was the true story behind American history.

"You called dude what again? Says the man name us H. Rap Brown." Ace turned the book toward him in case he'd mistaken it for something else.

"Al-Amin – Jamil Abdullah Al-Amin. When he converted to Islam in the seventies, he changed his name…"

"Why the book…"

"The book," Trigga read the confusion on Ace's face, "was published in 1969 – before the name change. But you never heard of Al-Amin? Like Al-Amin and the West End assassins?"

"West End assassins? Nah, never heard of 'em." Ace wondered when in the hell did the West End get some assassins.

"Damn, my boy lost in the sauce. When Al-Amin became the imam of the mosque of Atlanta, a few of his followers became serious devotees, handling whatever business Al-Amin thought necessary. In the eighties and nineties. they shut shit down over there in the West End. No dope selling, no robbing, raping, none of that shit. Even twelve had to put some respect on comrade. He'd gotten things under control for real. Then them crackers hated…" Trigga slid the water bottle across the counter to Ace, who could tell that he wasn't done.

Trigga continued after taking a sip from the juice. "In 2000, a couple of sheriffs pulled up on him about something, and shit got crazy. It's so many different versions of it that a nigga don't know what to believe. But when it was over, one sheriff had died, the other one was shot the fuck up too, but he made it – disappointingly. And Al-Amin, he wasn't hit period. Had made it out of Georgia before being caught four days later in Alabama."

"Damn…" The word slipped from Ace's lips unconsciously. Coincidentally, today was the fourth day of his own manhunt.

"How did they catch him?" Ace had to ask. It wasn't every day you picked up a book by an author whose story was very similar to your own.

"Shid, somehow, they found out that he was in Bama, where some of his relatives stayed, and caught him in woods close to there. I wished he wouldn't of stopped, just kept on going till he hit Texas or even farther. But then again, that still probably wouldn't have mattered. These crackers got eyes everywhere, from cameras to snitching ass people. A nigga can only run so long." Trigga looked at Ace seriously. He hated to see anybody in that type of predicament, running from the law which always seemed to catch up with the best of them. It reminded him of the stories from slavery. Black men running for their life because white men felt like they had a right to it. And he wanted to prove they didn't, which was why he'd help Ace.

"That's why ain running till Paul ass is in the ground and them diamonds are in my hand. Then, it ain't gonna matter how this shit end. I made my choices and going to continue to make 'em until a mutha-fucka put me in the dirt." Ace couldn't take Trigga's statement as a jab at his situation. He'd simply stated a fact no one could argue with. The United States government always got what they wanted – eventually.

Trigga smirked. "You keep mentioning these diamonds. Personally, I think your mind need to be on getting out of the country instead of traveling across it for something that may be a lot farther than you think." Trigga used a finger to snub the itch behind his ear. "You don't feel like you reaching?"

Ace wasn't about to argue his next course of actions. He'd follow it through – with or without Trigga.

"I'll see soon enough. And even if I wanted to leave the country, how would I do it? I'm the most famous person on this side of America right now. Every airport, train, and bus station is on the lookout for any red flag concerning me. I don't have a spare identity laying around somewhere. I'm stuck, so I'm going for what I know, and I know where those diamonds are located."

Trigga gulped down another swallow of the juice before looking at his watch. It was a little past midnight, and if he didn't want to bump heads with the wrath of his girlfriend, Ashley, he needed to be leaving now. "Ight, cool. If you feel like that's the best move for you, who am I to tell you different? But I got some connects who will build you a new identity for a good piece of change…"

"How much?" Ace questioned, cutting him off. If Trigga could get it done, that by itself would solve most of his problems.

"Nigga, do you got anything?"

"Yeah, about thirty…" Ace was ready to give all the money he had in exchange for the identity.

"That ain't close to being enough for the official-official. But we'll think of something. The room down the hall to the left is where you'll be sleeping. Make ya self at home and don't fuck up shit. Eat what you feel. It ain't no TVs here either, so when you get bored of thinking, pick up a book and learn something." Trigga smiled then disappeared down the short stairs they'd came up upon entering.

Ace glanced around his abode of silence, thankful for this moment of peace. The past four days hadn't allowed such a moment. He'd be a damn fool not to take advantage of it by getting as much rest as he could. Tomorrow and the days ahead were waiting.

Standing from the stool, he picked up Al-Amin's book again. "Might as well learn something," he said mockingly, heading down the hallway.

CHAPTER FIFTEEN

Kero

The two of them had been sitting in Kero's car for the past thirty minutes or so. Light drops of rain were falling from the grey sky overhead.

He quickly wiped away the lonely tear which broke itself free from the emotional build up he'd held since waking up this morning and those four mornings before.

This was the fifth day, approximately one hundred and seventeen hours, since he heard the distraught voice of his baby sister. Since he walked into her closet, finding her lifeless body.

He never imagined a day when his little Doll wouldn't be here – alive. A day when he couldn't tell her that he loved her and that he'd see her later.

Every right he once held to those simple gestures were forfeited and not to be regained. And all for what?

There were too many transgressions. Too many paths he'd crossed for him to just lay blame on one particular thing. But that was his karma – his alone. Fanny didn't deserve any of it.

Kero massaged the bridge of his nose to push away the tears dying to be freed. He shut his eyelids. The light taps of rain sent his mind reeling back to the day his course became set in stone.

"Fuck! This mutha…" Kero's heart beat harder than he thought it

could. Thanks to his quick reflexes and the other driver, the head-on collision was avoided. The smell of screeching tires found its way into the vents. Though he couldn't stop. His baby sister's life was on the line.

The car jumped the curb as he made a quick turn in front of Fanny's building. Grabbing the Millennium Nine from the seat, he hopped out and ran to her apartment. His pulse quickened as he neared the partially open door. He could hear a television playing, but that was it.

Forcefully, he pushed it open, sweeping the gun's sight across the space. No one was in the living room.

"Fanny!" he yelled, moving for the hallway. "Fanny!" Something was definitely wrong. The first bedroom door, he knocked open. His nephew wasn't in his room. Kero aimed the pistol at his sister's room across from him.

Did Ace take them? he wondered, calling her name again, then he yelled Ace's. Kero didn't know what type of game he was trying to play, but he'd be down for whatever once his sister and nephew were out of harm's way. He wouldn't hesitate to exchange his life for theirs.

Fanny's bedroom door was slightly ajar, so he peeked between the slit before easing it open. Empty. The bathroom was only a few steps farther. His gut feeling said they weren't here, but he needed to be sure.

Empty again.

"Ain't no way he took my sister." Kero roughly rubbed the pistol against the side of his face. He didn't know where to start to get them back.

Fuck! He'd fucked up badly this time.

Stopping in front of Fanny's room, he was trying to envision what happened. He could hear Fanny's delicate voice and Josh's cries then Ace's revengeful tone before the sharp shriek from his sister. The call ended.

Kero glanced around the room a second time, trying to think. For the first time, he noticed the closet. The door was partially open, and he knew why. How could he be so dumb to bring Ace's safe over here out of all the places in the world he should have taken it to?

But his stupid ass chose to bring it here, a place he knew Ace had knowledge of. Though he didn't think Ace would make it or go to this extent – just like he didn't think Ace would catch up to the DEA bitch and that she'd tell Ace about his role in the death of Sassy.

When Ariel unexpectedly left that morning, he quickly realized how much he'd underestimated Ace's ability to accomplish what seemed un-accomplishable. Although he hadn't worried about his or his sister's safety because it was understood that once he made the attempt to kill her, he'd be busy with trying to stay alive and free.

Swift told him that the shit he set in store for Ace and his little friend would have them searching for the deepest rabbit hole to bury themselves in. And that was if the mafia failed to take care of both of them first.

However, putting total belief in Swift's plans alone wasn't enough to assure him that they'd be cut out of the picture of life for good. There was another avenue just in case. Keith wanted revenge for his brother's death, and Kero paved a clear path for him. His luck, both traps had failed, and Ace was out for blood.

He stepped closer to the closet's door, unprepared for what he was about to find. Kero pulled it open.

"Fanny!" His heart fell to the pit of his stomach. "No, please no!" He dropped down to one knee. Immediately, he saw the flesh wound on the side of her head upon lifting her into his arms.

"Wake up, Fanny, please…" he begged, shaking her body. She wasn't dead, he kept telling himself, until he finally came to grips with their reality. Fanny wasn't waking up again.

Kero cried from the depths of his soul, rocking her back-and-forth. He screamed until his lungs burned for relief.

His thoughts were shattered pieces of vague memories scattered over the pit of his mental. There existed no word to describe the torture of this moment.

Blood continued to ooze slowly from her. She wasn't dead. "No, no, no…" Using his thumb, Kero tried to push the essence of her life back in. It was pointless – and he was left hopeless.

"I'm sorry," he muttered through trembling, tear-soaked lips. He had fucked up. Kero placed his head against her's. She wasn't dead.

Kero sat a moment longer before parting his eyelids. Five days ago, he'd found Fanny. This was the first time returning since then. He stared beyond the windshield, regretting the part he played in making his nephew motherless.

He could never make amends for it. Kero would hunt Ace, and until he caught up with him, he'd kill whatever family he had left. If he crossed paths with Ariel, she'd finally see all the things he wanted to do to her. Then, he'd kill her too.

However, those thoughts were for later. Right now, only two things needed to be in his mind. One was the words he'd use to express his deepest, apologetic condolences to his nephew. Two was to constantly remind himself that whatever his mother chose to say or dish out, he more than deserved. No matter how heavy the burden of his mother's attack became, out of respect for his sister, he would sit there and bear every ounce of her assault.

His mother lost her youngest child. Didn't she deserve to scorch every soul involved with nothing less than her furious rage? His lips were glued shut on the matter. And he was only doing it – again – out of respect for Fanny.

Kero exhaled a deep breath. Procrastination never got anything done. He opened his car door.

"Aye, I'ma go up there with you," Spain said, opening his door as well. For the past few days, he'd stuck close to Kero. He was anything but himself. Fanny's death drove him to a place Spain could only hope he'd return from soon. Kero was his brother, and he hated seeing how desolate and broken Ace caused him to become.

There was a time when Kero's very mouth spewed out so many words regarding Ace's reaction to his baby moms' death that Spain found himself in an awkward position. He looked up to Kero, but how was he supposed to compromise the heartless inscription of Kero's dogma?

Spain's recollections became the engraved scriptures of his memory, solely for him to recall when he needed guidance. Now, there sat the engraver, closely resembling the antagonistic aspects of his own work. Spain was at the beginning of understanding.

Kero said nothing in return, only nodded his head. His mother was waiting.

Leading Spain up to the door, Kero turned the knob, pushing it open. The first person he saw was his cousin, Evet. Her puffy face looked as if she'd been crying for days. Her and Fanny were past being close. They were each other's favorite family members.

Then there was Fred, who was of no *real* relation, yet he'd been a part of the family since Kero himself was a child. In the small kitchen sat his Auntie Marion who, even in old age, was still as beautiful as in her youth. Her older sister – who he purposely skipped – was the direct opposite of her. Josephine.

All of their eyes were sympathetic except for his mother's. Her glare bore daggers through him. The crack turned her face into that of a goblin. The structure of every bone and muscle was etched out in her skin. Her cloudy grey eyes spoke of pure hatred.

"Now, here his bitch ass is…" Josephine pulled on her cigarette, letting the smoke exit her nostrils like a dragon.

"Josephine, don't. That boy hurt like we all is," his auntie said in his defense. She had always wa…

"Hurrrrt?" Josephine smacked her teeth. "Why he hurt? He the muthafucka that done it," she said with the jerk of her hand.

"Hush, Josephine." His auntie walked over and gave him a hug. "I know it's hurting, baby. But God got a better plan for her. I promise you…"

His mother laughed sarcastically. *"God got a better plan for her? Bitch, don't start that shit."*

"I told you to watch your mouth when you talking to me." Auntie Marion jabbed her finger at Josephine as she spoke. Out of everybody in their family, Auntie Marion was the only one that kept her older sister in her place. Yes, she was a God-fearing woman, but she hadn't been brought up in God's house. In her day, her and her sister were known as the *Brawling Bitches from Bixby*.

"Bitch, whateva," Josephine returned before taking a gulp from the bottle of gin. "Now move yo ass out the way so I can talk to my pussy ass boy."

Instinctively, Kero's jaw tightened. This was why he never came around her. Her fucking mouth. Again, out of respect for Fanny. He noticed something was missing.

"Where Josh?" Kero asked, looking at Evet.

Before she could, his mother answered. "Why the fuck you wanna know, so you can kill him too? Muthafucka, you will never see that boy again!"

"Josephine!" Marion was getting fed up.

"*Marion!*" she mocked and giggled. "But okay, I tell you what, boy. Tell me what the fuck happened to my baby, and I might think about it."

"Josephine…"

"Shhhh! Let the boy speak now. We all need to hear this." She gestured with her hand for him to answer. Kero stood there, staring her dead in the eyes. If she already knew that he – somehow – was involved, why should he admit to it? She didn't deserve the satisfaction.

"I don't know wh…"

"See, that's guilt. Marion, I told you his bitch ass was gonna lie…"

"Oh, shut up. You ain't thinking right now with all that devil's juice poisoning ya." Marion extended the cup of water she'd poured. He refused. "Don't pay yo mama no mind. She feeling what we all is…"

"No, y'all muthafuckas feeling sorry and shit. Bitch, I'm angry and want some damn answers."

This was the first time in years he'd seen tears streak his mother's face. The only other time was when she'd brought Fanny into the world. Back then, his mother shared the same light as *Wonder Woman*. But crack changed her.

"See-see, I find it funny that you had managed to make it here before the police. The police said when they walked in, you were crying like a little bitch, holding my baby with yo dirty ass hands. They say you laid a gun on the floor – and I laughed and told that man that my son always carry guns, Mr. Officer.

"Then that son of a bitch had the nerve to ask did my baby deal in drugs. I stopped his ass right in his tracks. I said, 'First, don't everrr disrespect my baby and – no! She do not deal nor do drugs. Never have. Now my son, that's his thing. And I do enough drugs for the whole damn family.'" She laughed.

"But I was thinking to myself about what the girl said across the way. She heard a car sounded like it was about to crash. Then she saw you run in here with ya gun in hand. I said, 'Josephine, that fucker had that gun because he knew Fanny was in trouble. He knew that something was happening to her.'" She sniffed and took another sip, wiping away the flowing rivers of her pain.

Abruptly, she slammed the bottle down hard enough to crack the plastic table and cause everyone to jump. "Explain, muthafucka!"

All eyes were set on him. Auntie Marion wore an expression that said he'd have to tough this one out. He felt like a podium, motionless and at the center of attention. "She called me…" The crying began to replay in his ears.

"She called…" Josephine was impatiently waiting on the rest.

"She called me crying. I had missed all her messages. When I answered, she was trying to say something, but Josh was yelling in the background… I–I couldn't really hear her. Then someone took the phone from her…"

"Now, how did we get to this point?" He could still hear Ace as clear as the day.

Josephine appeared to be locked on each word which fell from his lips, like she was concentrating on memorizing every single one.

Kero dropped his head, scratching the side of his face. He didn't know where to take the story from here. He wouldn't give her the satisfaction.

Finally, his Uncle Fred broke the momentary silence. "What was said?" The question was asked like they all had it on their minds. Besides him stood Spain, who he forgot was standing right behind him. He was the only person he'd told what Ace said – and would continue to be the only person.

Kero gritted his teeth. "The nigga said he wanted money – and I gave him the code to the safe."

Josephine pulled on the cigarette hard. Her eyes narrowed. "He wanted more than damn money. The officer said there were two safes in there. That's why they wanna say it was drugs. Now, tell me who shit you stole because that damn sure wasn't yo safe."

"Josephine, stop accusing him. You don't know if it was his or not." His auntie was back on his side.

"I do know. I was over here two days before she died. I was back there in the closet and saw both of them. When I asked her why this bitch-made ass nigga had two safes, she said that *new* one, he brought the day before that. I asked what he had in there cause I told him to his face not to have no damn drugs around my grandbaby. But she didn't know, and he didn't give her the code to find out."

Josephine pointed the cigarette at him. "Why didn't you? You trusted that girl with everything but not the code to that safe because I bet you didn't know it. Now, I'ma ask yo trifling ass one more time who shit got my baby killed. And you betta think real long and hard about it cause if you don't tell me the truth, you can bet your black ass that the police gon get it out of you once I tell them that muthafucka was stolen from the person who killed my baby, and my fucking son know who it is because he *stole it!*" After yelling the last two words, Josephine took a large gulp, disgusted that he came out of her pussy.

She stared daggers into him. "I wish I would of swallowed you, punk muthafucka."

"Shut up!" Marion barked.

After letting out a loud belch, she continued. "Who you think gonna be their number one suspect then? But you know what..." Josephine took a long drag from the remainder of the cigarette then dossed it in the cup of beer she'd been done with.

"I don't even wanna know because you," she jabbed a finger at Kero, "you the reason they did this, you the reason they took my baby, and you betta fucking finish it." Taking a quick sip from the bottle of gin again, Kero's mother came to her feet with a demonic expression – as if she was possessed. "I don't give a flying fuck how. You betta make them pay for what they did to my baby!" she screamed at the top of her lungs. Tears relentlessly poured down her face as she stepped within reach of her son.

"You hear me, pussy muthafucka!" No one in the room was prepared for the swift slap Josephine delivered to Kero's face. "You betta fucking kill them!" she cried, repeatedly throwing slap, after slap – hit after hit – until Uncle Fred grabbed her at Marion's frantic request.

Kero stood there, talking every lick his mother chose. Plenty of times he'd cursed his mother, slammed doors in her face, punched holes in her walls, but never had he laid hands on her. Never would he disrespect the woman who brought him into this world that way. For years, he'd been her personal punching bag whenever she raged in a drunken fit for reasons only Josephine knew. Though today, they both knew why.

This was why – right now – he failed to dodge any of her furious blows. He more than deserved it. His actions had led to his mother's child's death – his baby sister. Regardless of if he didn't think Ace would take it that far, Kero was the one to put her in the middle of some street shit which had nothing to do with her.

"You betta make 'em pay!" His grieving mother screamed as Uncle Fred was finally able to wrap his arms around her and pull her back. Auntie Marion unhesitatingly attempted to check the damage, but Kero turned, refusing her care.

"Kennedy, don't be like that. She just grieving." Placing an arm around his shoulder, she lightly squeezed him closer. "Y'all got to get it together for Katie," Marion said, using both of their real names like she always had. Kero hadn't heard the name in so long that it sounded almost foreign to him.

"I'm good, Auntie…" he told her before turning to leave. The words from his mother continued to ring loudly in his ears. *"You betta make 'em pay!"* The intensity of his burning revenge began to ascend within him. For five days, he had cried, cursed, and cried more. Nothing would replace the life of his little sister. Nothing could bring her back. This very moment would be the same for the rest of his life.

His hands balled into tight fists. Coming from under the shade of the hallway, Kero stepped out into the drizzling drops from above. The rain washed over his face, merging with the tears he wasn't able to control. His mother made it clear that the light of both of their lives was gone, never to return.

In his peripheral, he noticed Spain getting into the car, though he chose to stand in the rain a few more minutes. Badly, he wanted it to wash away his pain – the faults of his own desire. But he knew neither of those would free him from their piercing claws unless he did what was supposed to be done more than a year ago – cause the death of Ace.

At the moment, he didn't know exactly how he'd get it done. Ace was a wanted man who could be anywhere by now. This was what was making Kero lose his mind. How in the hell was he to find a nigga hiding from damn near everything?

For the first time, he remembered something long forgotten.

"That's my way," Kero said to himself, wiping his face after he'd gotten into the car as well.

"You good?" Spain asked, really lost on what else to say, especially after the tirade of Ms. Josephine. That wasn't his first time seeing her lose it on Kero. Though it was a first for him to see the lady so broken, so miserable – so right. Somehow, she'd hit the nail on the head, and he knew that by itself fucked with Kero the most because it was true. He was the reason Ace reacted the way he did.

"I'll never be until this nigga dead," Kero snarled. Within that very instant, his phone started buzzing.

He glanced at it. "This fuck nigga," he grumbled, dropping the cell back to the cupholder. Keith had been calling for the last few days, and Kero had faithfully ignored every call. He'd lost his sister, and whatever the fuck Keith wanted, he'd hav…

A sudden thought came to Kero's mind. Maybe it was time to stop avoiding his calls.

CHAPTER SIXTEEN

Ace

The field stretched endlessly, grass swaying in a light breeze Ace couldn't feel. The world was still, like it was holding its breath, watching. Beside him, Missy sat in quiet elegance, dressed in the soft colors of a past he could never return to.

Out in the distance, the land broke into water, a lake, dark and restless beneath the weight of a storm that churned only above it. Thick, black clouds hung low, and rain fell in violently, drowning the lake in sorrow. But nowhere else did the rain fall. The storm wept for one place alone.

Ace let his eyes linger on it, his voice heavy when he finally spoke. "I wish I could come see you."

Missy turned her head slightly, studying him the way only a mother could. Ace didn't look at her. Couldn't. His eyes stayed on that storm, like something in it reflected the storm in him.

"But I can't," he continued, jaw tightening. "My enemies stacked the odds against me."

Missy exhaled softly, not with sadness but with knowing. "Enemies," she said, "are what kingdoms are made of."

Ace frowned, finally looking at her. Her face was the same as he remembered, strong, warm – eternal.

"Without them, how would a king prove his might?" she asked, tilting her head. "How would he prove his right to rule the lands?"

Ace turned back to the storm, his fists clenching onto his lap. Thunder rumbled deep within his chest, as if it had crawled inside him and made a home there.

"I don't want to rule lands," he said, voice rough. "I just want revenge. For Whiteboy. For Sassy. For Dre."

A loud crack of lightning split the sky. The lake, already swollen, rippled violently as the rain poured harder, its surface growing wild, angry, uncontainable – just like him.

Missy's smile faded. Her eyes, still soft, now carried something deeper. She raised a hand and gestured toward the lake.

"I can see the pain," she murmured. "Because your tears are flooding your soul with sorrow."

Ace's breath hitched. He hadn't cried. He hated crying. But when he looked at the storm again, he saw it, his pain made real, falling from the sky, sinking into the earth, drowning him inch by inch.

Missy turned her gaze back to him, watching his silence stretch between them like a canyon.

"Is this what you want?" she asked.

Ace didn't answer. Because this wasn't about what he wanted. It was about what had to be done.

Missy sighed. This time, there was no softness in it. No warmth. It was the sigh of a woman who had seen too much, understood too much. When she spoke, her voice held the weight of truth.

"Baby, if your sacrifice is worth it, then make sure you gain the most from it."

Ace swallowed, his heartbeat steady and cold.

"The best revenge," Missy continued, "is when the enemy kills himself for you."

Thunder crashed over the lake. The storm continued to spread. The rain kept falling. And somewhere deep inside him, Ace felt the flood rise.

It was 8:21 in the a.m. when Ace woke up. He laid in the bed, trying to beat back the thudding ache of his forehead.

He couldn't remember the last time he'd thought about his dying mother. He wondered had she saw her only son's face all over the news.

Ace sat on the edge of the bed, staring out of the small window that let in a sliver of light. His eyes blurred as he drifted back to the memory of Missy, the woman who had given him life, who was slowly being taken by the crushing force of cancer. He could still see her fragile, beautiful face that once had been so full of strength, even as the disease consumed her. He could still hear her voice in his head, telling him, *"The best revenge is when the enemy kills himself for you…"*

His thoughts shifted, like they always did when the pain of losing her became too much.

Trigga. The man had left him alone for five days now, only checking in occasionally to make sure Ace hadn't thought of anything stupid. Every time he called, the instructions were the same. "Chill. Wait. Keep your head down. You gotta know this shit gonna take a minute."

It felt like everything was on hold, like Ace was stuck in a holding pattern, waiting for something to change, waiting for something to happen. But Ace didn't have time for that.

Finally, he heard the sound of a knock at the door. He stood up, not needing to ask who it was. He already knew.

Trigga walked in, his eyes scanning the house before resting on Ace. His face was hard, like stone, but Ace could see the flicker of something beneath that facade. There was some kind of glimmer in his eye that spoke of something Ace couldn't quite figure out.

"I'm still here, waiting," Ace muttered, leaning against the wall. "We don't have time to be sitting idle. The clock's ticking."

Trigga's expression remained unchanged, but there was a faint shrug. "The fake docs take time, Ace," he said. "And *you* don't have enough to make it happen yet."

Ace clenched his fists, frustrated. "So, what now? I'ma just sit here and wait until I have enough? I'm not that patient, nigga."

Trigga stepped forward, pulling a stool and sitting down. His posture was confident, his voice calm. "Nah, we're not sitting. We're strategizing." He pulled out a small notebook, flipping through pages.

"I'm saying, you trying to handle Paul, right? So, we need to move like we're on a chessboard. Ever play before?"

Ace's brow furrowed, a mix of confusion and irritation flashing across his face. "No," he muttered. "Never cared for it." He wondered why this nigga was *so* into giving lessons.

Trigga nodded, his voice low but serious. "Alright, let me break it down for you. Paul's the king. The king is the most important piece on the board, but he's always protected. Around him, you've got your knights, rooks, bishops – his trusted men. Every piece on that board is working to protect the king, keep him safe, secure."

He paused for a moment, letting the words settle in. "But the real key to the game is the pawns. The pawns are the ones who get moved first, the ones who matter most. Without the pawns, the king's open for the taking. So, that's where we're starting."

Ace's eyes narrowed. "The pawns. Got it."

Trigga leaned forward. "Now, listen. We need to hit the pawns, the small players in his network. But that's not the end game. It's just the beginning. We hit them, get what we need to move forward, and then we'll figure out how to make the rest of the pieces fall into place."

Ace listened, taking in the weight of the plan. Then, Trigga glanced up at Ace. When he'd finally finished, he told Ace, "Put on that synthetic disguise, and I'll show you how we get the rest of the bread to pay for those docs."

About an hour later, Ace and Trigga were in Trigga's tinted-out car, the engine roaring as they cruised down the street. Ace had switched into his disguise, his features hidden behind a thick set of fake facial hair and dreads and a new demeanor. They were headed toward one of the Manterio family's luxury car dealerships, part of the empire Paul had built and a key piece in Trigga's plan.

As they approached, Trigga's eyes narrowed. The dealership was luxurious, its glass windows reflecting the pale light of day, its marble floors hidden behind expensive cars on display. But something caught Trigga's attention.

"Now look at that," he muttered. "The van's here."

The Manterio family's carrier van, with Stockage Plaza printed on the side, was parked in front, idling quietly as two men loaded boxes, likely filled with cash or some other form of valuables. At the front of the vehicle, a man stood guard, his posture rigid, scanning the area for any signs of a threat.

Ace glanced around, realizing an open opportunity. "This is it. Shid, we can make our move now. Shit sweet." Ace's eyes locked onto the scene, every part of him beginning to calculate every option. This was their chance – the next step in their plan. It was time to make the pawns move.

Ace's jaw clenched, his fists tightening as he stared at the idling van. The opportunity was sitting right there.

"I can take this now," Ace said, his voice sharp with urgency.

Trigga didn't move. His grip on the steering wheel tightened. "Nah, we can't. Nigga, we ain't prepared to take this right now, Ace. Where we taking the van? We don't got a spot for it, and on top of that, we in my *real* car."

Ace didn't care about any of that. His mind was set. "Drive down the street then. I'm not letting this pass. You said the money in the vans, and it's a damn van right here." His eyes remained locked on their lunch.

Trigga threw him a skeptical look. "The fuck you mean drive down the street?"

Ace turned to him, his expression stone cold, his patience thin. "Look, either you take me down the street to drop me off or I'm getting out right here and taking that van."

Trigga exhaled sharply, shaking his head. "Man, this is wild."

Ace leaned in slightly, his voice lowering, making sure Trigga felt every word. "I got nothing to lose. If there's money in that van, that's my ticket. I ain't letting it slip."

They stared at each other for a moment; a silent war of wills raged between them. Then, Trigga cursed under his breath, putting the car in gear and pulling out of the Classic Cushion parking lot next to the luxury dealership. He didn't speed, didn't make any sudden movements, just drove like it was another normal night on the street.

As they neared the spot, he finally asked Ace, "You serious about this?"

Ace glanced at him then at the van in the side mirror. His voice was steady, unwavering. "You said it yourself – it's only so long a nigga can run. I might as well make the most of it."

Trigga sucked his teeth, gripping the wheel tighter as he eased the vehicle down the street and to a stop.

Ace popped the door open, his heart already pounding, but his mind? Cold. Focused. Ready. He stepped out – his stride quick, calculated – heading up the sidewalk toward the dealership. He had one shot, and that was all he needed.

Ace treaded quickly up the short walk to the edge of the parking lot as his mind started to race. A few workers were tying down furniture in Classic Cushion's parking lot, oblivious to what was about to unfold. The van was still idling. The guard was still posted out front, scanning the lot.

Ace was trying to think about the different ways to play it, but there was no time – no second guessing. He walked straight for the man.

The guard's head snapped toward him, his posture stiffening. He barely had time to react before…

BOOM! BOOM!

Ace's gun barked twice, the bullets slamming into the man's chest. The guard staggered back, the impact absorbed by a vest he had on. Ace didn't hesitate sending the third slug toward his face.

Chaos erupted. A few workers near Classic Cushions scrambled inside, shouting. A man loading a box into the van dropped it, reaching for a gun at his waist, but Ace was already moving.

He dove into the van, yanking the door shut as he swung the gun up, letting two fast shots fly through the side window, forcing the gunman to duck behind a door of the dealership.

Before he could let off another round, Ace slammed the van into gear and punched the gas. Tires screeched, and the van lurched forward, cutting hard onto the street as a few boxes toppled out the back, spilling onto the pavement.

He flew from the dealership, eyes cutting to the side mirror. There was no immediate chase, but that wouldn't last long.

A car appeared in the distance – coming fast. *Trigga.* Ace yanked the wheel, jerking the van into a side street. As he slowed for just a second, he hopped out, moving to the back. The doors swung open, boxes still inside.

Trigga's car pulled up alongside him. His window slid down just enough. "Follow me!"

With no hesitation, Ace slammed the doors shut, lunged back into the driver's seat, and hit the gas.

They tore off toward the expressway where there was no turning back.

They'd been driving hard for ten minutes, weaving from the expressway, through streets, before Trigga's car pulled up to the front of a vacant warehouse.

Ace looked at the rundown structure with rusted loading docks and busted-out windows. Perfect. He drove the van into the building's interior, tires kicking up dust as he skidded to a stop.

Trigga had already jumped out. "We gotta unload this shit now. The van got a tracker on it."

Ace nodded, jumping into the back of the van as Trigga climbed up beside him. Without hesitation, both started shoving the remaining boxes out, letting them crash onto the concrete. Some tumbled, one busting open. Stock exchange books spilled out.

Ace frowned. "The fuck?" Before the thought could settle, another box flipped open upon impact, and this time, bundles of tightly wrapped cash slid across the ground.

Ace froze, his breath stopping. Stacks on stacks, sealed tight, came from under the books.

Trigga let out a low whistle but didn't waste time staring. After tossing the last box out, Trigga said, "Yo, get that van the fuck outta here now!"

Snapping back, Ace ran back in the driver's seat, threw the van in gear, and peeled out. Trigga followed close behind, headlights bouncing in the rearview.

Seven minutes later, they found a secluded area, which was perfect for dumping the van. Ace rolled the vehicle into a dirt-covered alleyway, killed the engine, and hopped out. He pushed the door open, making sure nothing was left behind. Then, without a word, he slid into Trigga's passenger seat.

They left the van behind to be somebody else's problem.

～

Ace sat back in the chair, grinning as his fingers drummed against the stacks of cash piled up on the table. The dim light overhead flickered, casting shadows over the bundles – close to seven hundred thousand just for taking the van. He couldn't believe it, but the proof was right in front of him. This wasn't just a fluke. It was an opportunity.

He shook his head, still half in disbelief. "Damn… maybe I don't need to cross the country. Maybe these plans you got gonna work and get a nigga everything I really need. And that muthafucka head." His voice was leveled, as if speaking the thought aloud might make it more real.

Trigga smirked, leaning forward with his elbows on his knees. He was calm, playing the perfect chess player in this whole game. "But the thing about chess, homie, is that he'll get his chance to move. They'll change shit up a little. That was just the first play. You got a lot more pieces to move before you can get a checkmate."

Ace's eyes flickered with fire, like the storm inside him had sparked anew. His hand rested over the bundles of cash, but his mind was elsewhere, spinning faster than he could track. He didn't care about the game anymore; he didn't care about the moves. What he wanted now was to hurt Paul in every possible way he could.

He leaned forward, locking eyes with Trigga. "Okay, well, I wanna know the rest of it. I want more money… and I want Paul dead. For Whiteboy. I'm ready to take all his shit and burn his name into the concrete of the streets. I'm done waiting. Fuck waiting. That was a move, and why wait on his? Nigga, fuck 'em. Let's jus take it however it come, without the wait. He can't react to everything."

Trigga met his gaze, his face serious now, the usual smirk gone. There was something deeper in his eyes, a quiet understanding of just how far Ace was willing to go. He nodded slowly, the wheels turning in his head. "Good. You're ready. That hunger you got? That's what's gonna make us win. But just remember – revenge is a heavy price to pay. You want to end Paul's life, you gotta line that muthafucka up in ya sight. Then you hit him where he thinks he's bulletproof."

Ace's fingers tightened around a stack of cash, his expression hardening. "Then let's hit him hard. I don't care about his empire or his people. I just want him gone. No more lies. No more games."

Trigga sat back, a slow smile spreading across his face as he saw the fire in Ace's eyes. "Shid, say no more. Check this out. Paul's got his people, yeah. His pawns and his knights. But he's a king, and he thinks he's untouchable. He hides behind his money, his businesses, and his guards. He's surrounded himself with all this power. But what happens when the king has no control over his own pieces? What happens when the pawns start moving on their own?"

Ace's breath quickened. He was following, feeling the plan start to take shape in his mind. "I'm listening."

Trigga leaned forward a little more, tapping a finger on the table, drawing invisible lines in the air as he spoke. "Paul's used to being the one who's clipping strings. But you know what? We're gonna flip the board on him. We start with the people closest to him. The ones he knows are loyal, the ones he's using. The same people who are scared of him but still want a piece of the game. We hit them first. Break the foundation. That's where the real power lies."

Ace narrowed his eyes, seeing where this was going. "So, we hit who first? We make them bleed first. I'm down with sending a few messages."

Trigga nodded, grinning now. "Now we on the same fucking page. We send him a messages. We hit his people, one by one, until he has no choice but to come out and deal with us. And when he does? That's when we finish it. When he's desperate, when he thinks he can't allow this to go on any further. That's when *you* strike for the kill."

Ace's pulse quickened. He felt the rage bubbling up again, stronger this time, deadlier. "Where do we start next? I don't care about the place, time, or day. I want him to feel every single piece of what I do. For Whiteboy… For everything."

Trigga met his gaze, his voice steady but serious now. "If you're ready to go all the way, Ace, then you need to understand this. The next round a be a bit more to chew. We make Paul destroy everything he built, and by the time we finish, he'll have no choice but to fall the fuck over. Checkmate."

Ace leaned back, the weight of the plan sinking in. "I like it. I'm in. Let's do it."

Trigga nodded, satisfied. "Aight then. We got the guns. We got the plan. We start moving the pieces tomorrow. The first move? We hit one of his best players. We shake up the ground beneath him, make him feel like everything he's built is crumbling."

Ace stood up, pacing the room as the adrenaline surged through him. "I'm ready. I'll take out every single one of them. I don't care who they are. I wanna make this whole city bleed until Paul feels it. I won't stop until he's gone."

Trigga followed his every movement with a steady gaze, knowing this was it, the moment when everything would either fall into place or spiral out of control. But Trigga wasn't worried. He'd seen this kind of hunger before.

"That's the energy we need, Ace. Let's make it count."

CHAPTER SEVENTEEN

Trigga

Trigga stepped out of the house, pulling the door shut behind him. The weight of the night seemed lighter on him. He took a quick glance at the window, making sure Ace wasn't looking out as he headed for his car

Sliding in, he exhaled, gripping the steering wheel as he reached into his pocket. His fingers found his phone, and in one swift motion, he unlocked it and dialed a number he had memorized long ago.

The line rang twice. Then a voice, deep and steady.

"Yeah..."

Trigga rested his head against the seat, his free hand drumming against his thigh. "How much we talkin for that info?" His voice was calm, but there was an edge to it, a quiet urgency.

The other end hesitated for a second before murmuring something low. Trigga listened, his grip on the steering wheel tightening. Numbers. Conditions. He could hear the greed woven into the words. These kinds of people never gave up anything for free.

He let them talk, his expression unreadable, then cut in smoothly. "All that'll happen once you tell me a ticket that's worth my while."

Silence. Then a low chuckle. "We'll be in touch." The line went dead.

Trigga let the phone rest on his lap as he stared out through the windshield. The street ahead was still, but his mind wasn't. He tapped his fingers against the steering wheel, his thoughts piecing together the next steps.

Ace was about to solve everything. Whether he realized it or not, he was the last piece needed to put the game in motion. The money, the blood, the revenge, it was all lining up.

Trigga smirked to himself, shaking his head.

"It's almost time."

Then, he put the car in drive and disappeared into the night.

CHAPTER EIGHTEEN

Whiteboy

"Fuck!" Whiteboy growled under his breath, pushing forward through the dimly lit corridor. The walls were grimy, the air thick with the scent of mildew and dust, but none of that mattered. What mattered was getting out. He moved with purpose, glancing back every few steps to make sure no one was following him. More importantly, he needed to be sure he wasn't leaving behind a telltale trail of blood.

Nobody. No blood. Good so far.

His right hand pressed against the wound beneath his clothing, fingers slick with blood. He had no clue how much damage was done. He wasn't a doctor, but the pain was defining and throbbing with each heartbeat. A hospital was out of the question. That was a death trap. There was no telling who might be waiting for him there. Cops. Enemies.

Whiteboy pushed forward, his breath tight in his throat. At the end of the corridor, he stopped. Listened. The silence did all but ease the evident tension. Then, he chanced a glance around the corner, one eye peeking past the edge of the wall.

A woman's scream shattered the quiet. "Oh, my God!"

He didn't need to look to know what she had seen. What they had started, he had finished.

The body laid behind him, lifeless. Blood pooled around it, soaking into the cracked concrete floor. The sight of it had frozen her in place but not for long.

Whiteboy didn't hesitate. The scream meant only one thing. The police were coming. No, correction. They were already on the way.

He pushed forward, biting down on the pain that shot through his ribs with every step. His only option now was to disappear.

He bent the corner, placing his armed hand into his left pocket. His eyes quickly swept across the parking area as he moved quickly along the walkway, searching for both enemies and transportation.

Time was of the essence. At any minute, it could all be over, both his freedom and life. At this point, both were very attractive.

He continued to move, glancing over his shoulder every few steps. *Fuck,* he cursed himself for being in such a rush that he'd forgotten the rental car's key. He realized this upon reaching the vehicle, something he could not go back and retrieve.

Now, he wondered which mistake weighed more on the harmful scale. Forgetting the key or not going back for the *damn key*.

Damn, he needed to think of something quick because there was no way in hell he'd make it out of the vicinity before Dekalb County police showed up.

"Fuck!" he slowly growled a third time, letting his retinas sweep over the scenery once more. Still nothing.

His gait slowed helplessly. What the fuck was he about to do now? Then, his ears caught the sound of sirens off in the distance. Now things were definitely worser.

Stepping from the walkway, he slid between a car and a van. wishing like hell at this very moment that he knew how to peel steering columns. If he made it out of this, he would acquire it as a skill of necessity. But it seemed to be a long shot at this instant.

He continued on, making it to the rear of the van, about to make his way across the parking lot. But he halted his movement. The rays of headlights flashed over the darkened center of the aisle and quickly beamed toward his way and out of sight.

Thank you, street God, he was thinking, speedily trotting in the direction of the parking space he'd seen his last hope swerve into.

Bringing the pistol from his pocket, he inched forward, eyeing his prey through the window of others' cars. There were two individuals within the highlighted interior.

He watched as they shuffled around, both getting out, gathering miscellaneous items. Then, both doors opened in unison. Even though it was dark out, he could tell that the driver was a female and the passenger a male. Both of them prey.

Quickly and silently, he moved closer, heading straight up the side of their car toward the girl.

"Say…" he growled, aiming the pistol at the female.

Startled, they both turned toward him. "Oh, shh…" the girl began but was quickly silenced.

"Shut the fuck up and get in…" he said, gesturing with the pistol toward the car.

"Aye, bra, man, whatever you want, you got it, just let us go," the guy pleaded, looking as if he was about to come around the vehicle to rescue her.

"Nigga, stop or I'ma slump both of y'all. Now get the fuck in the car." He watched then shared a look with the female before she did as told.

The girl slid in as if that was the last thing she wanted to do. "Stop…" he told her. "I want him to get in first."

They watched him get in. "Open the back door." Whiteboy took a step backwards, giving her enough room to act out his wishes.

"Now, hit the locks." She seemed reluctant to but did. "Get in…"

Once he slammed her door, he got in, placing the gun to the back of her headrest. He only freed his hand from the wound to shut his door.

"Ight, let's pull."

"Huh?" the girl questioned retardedly, like she was dumbfounded on what he actually meant. He was on the verge of explaining what he meant another way, but her boyfriend did it for him.

"Man, crank the car up and go."

"Exactly…" He could hear that the sirens were a lot closer now – way closer than they were seconds ago.

She maneuvered the car to the entrance of the parking lot. "Where are we going?"

"Go to the right and far away from here," Whiteboy told her, tapping the window with the gun at the direction where the police sirens were coming down the street. From what he could tell, there had to be at least fifteen to twenty cars heading their way.

All praise to Allah.

He waited a couple of minutes then glanced backwards to make sure they were only going after their designated location instead of after the vehicle which they'd missed by a second or two. And they had without the smallest impression that the entire street was a target area for their suspect.

After a couple of minutes, his breathing became steady despite the fire burning in his side. Every second felt stretched, the distant wail of sirens creeping closer, bouncing off the buildings like a warning shot. He forced himself to stay still, muscles tense, watching. Then, he glanced backward.

The cops had blown right past the car he was in. Their focus was too locked on their designated location. No hesitation. No suspicion. They had no idea the entire damn street was a war zone, a hunting ground where he had barely escaped being the prey.

A slow, relieved smile tugged at the corner of his lips. *How the fuck did I just pull off the impossible?*

Well, half the impossible. The ache in his torso quickly reminded him that he wasn't in the clear just yet. Whiteboy could still feel a river of blood spilling down his body, soaking into his clothes, becoming warm and sticky against his skin. He adjusted his grip over the wound, fingers pressing tight, but it didn't stop the relentless ebb.

Damn. Where is a doctor when you need one?

Every pulse of pain threatened to slow him down but stopping wasn't an option. He needed to move. Fast.

The shadows of the city stretched long under the flickering streetlights as the vehicle continued on. His mind began racing over his options. Hospitals were out, *too* risky. A back alley doc? Maybe – if he could make it to one before the blood loss took its toll. Or maybe he'd just have to patch himself up and pray he didn't bleed out before sunrise.

"Aye, bra – look, shawty, whatever you want, we'll give it to you. Shid, just take the car and let us out, my nigga." The guy said it as if he'd been through this type of situation a few times. His calm demeanor said it all.

"I only need a ride," he told them, removing the phone from his pocket.

"A ride? Where?" the guy asked, a little incredulously.

"*Damn*," he huffed sotto voice after realizing that he wouldn't be able to call out using his unarmed hand, which smeared blood across the screen.

Quickly, he swapped the gun and phone, letting the pistol rest on his knees while he wiped the phone against his other. He called the last number he'd hit then listened to the ring back, telling the guy, "I have no fucking idea."

The statement had caused reality to set in a little deeper than he really needed it to. He was close to being fucked.

"Shhh…" Whiteboy let out after getting the voicemail, the last thing he needed right now. He called again.

"What? You want us to just drive you around?" the guy asked, gazing over at his girl, who glanced in the rearview at Whiteboy every few seconds.

Her glances and his questions were both irritating the shit out of him. Now wasn't the time for questions or any funny shit.

"Yeah, until I find out where the hell y'all dropping me off at." He hoped his words would ease their fears and erase all thoughts of stupidity they likely were conjuring within their minds at this very moment.

He got the voicemail again. *Damn.* He hoped nothing had happened to the only person – and only family – he had.

Fuck. This was another 'last thing' he needed. He hoped his reason for not picking up at a time like this wasn't due to him being subjected to an ambush as well. That would make matters worse.

Finding another number, he lightly pressed the call icon.

It took five seconds for the other end to answer. "Hello…"

"Hey, where bra?" he asked, glancing out at the nights sky above, praying this would take his mind off of the painful wound releasing the flow of his life – whatever was left of it.

"Damn, I don't know. Twelve showed up, and I'm moving..." Whiteboy said into the phone, clenching his jaw. He could feel his shoulder beginning to numb along with the left side of his chest. His predicament was becoming more worse by the second.

"Yeah, in the shoulder and – and I think the si..." he was saying until the phone beeped. *Damn*, he thought, watching the warning signal of the battery dying.

"You shot?" the guy questioned, obviously a bit skeptical by this new revelation.

Whiteboy ignored him. "I'm good though but see where he at. I'ma try to make it to close to there, so I can get some help. I'll hit you when..." *Shit!* The phone powered off.

He tucked the dead device back into his pocket. The gun went back to his left hand, and his other hand went back to his wound. He closed his eyes for a moment, contemplating as to whether or not he'd chosen the right decision seconds ago.

Yet, then again, what other choice did he have right now? He was spewing out fluid like a Greek fountain, and hopefully he'd make it to his Ack before it ended up being too late!

"Say..." he began, pulling the small tote bag from around his shoulder. "Go to the West End and I'ma direct you from there. Here." Whiteboy pulled two rings from the bag.

The guy hesitated a moment before finally craning his head toward him. "What's this?" he questioned as his passenger handed over the two pieces.

"A small payment for the ride and a token of appreciation for *both* of y'all. Just take me where I need to be with no extra shit, aight?"

"Aight." The guy turned back around, inspecting the small tokens. He wanted to say *What the fuck?* but thought better not to.

The next sixteen minutes of the ride were in silence and peaceful – a little too peaceful for comfort.

He badly wanted to rest, but his paranoia had kicked into overdrive. Every instinct screamed at him to stay awake. To stay alert.

Here he was, bleeding out in the backseat of a car with two terrified individuals he'd essentially kidnapped. Blood poured from him, soaking into the seats. He felt himself slipping, body growing weaker by the second. He needed a plan, a destination, but still, he couldn't go to a hospital. Again, he was America's most wanted.

The odds were stacked against him.

"Where to?" the female asked, finally breaking the silence.

Whiteboy blinked, snapping back from the fog of his thoughts. His vision blurred for a second before he forced himself to focus. The streetlights outside flashed past in quick intervals, throwing jagged shadows across the interior.

Where the fuck are we…

He glanced around, trying to get himself together. He recognized the area, barely. Forming a coherent thought was getting harder. His fingers loosened over the wound, his breathing slowing. The world started to tilt.

A wave of dizziness crashed over him, and before he could stop it, darkness closed in.

Then everything faded to black.

The masked man's laughter echoed through the room, twisted and cruel. The cold steel of his gun wavered between the trembling woman in his grip and the man bleeding out on the floor.

"So now, tell me, which do you choose? Her or him?"

The words slithered from his mouth, thick with mockery. He was toying with Whiteboy, savoring the moment, knowing the torment of an impossible choice would eat him alive.

Whiteboy's grip tightened around his own gun, his pulse hammering against his skull. Sweat trickled down his temple as he tried to steady his aim. One shot. He needed one clean shot. But the girl was too close. One wrong move and she'd be the one to drop.

His breath heightened. They came all this way for her. His brother had died trying to save her.

His teeth clenched so hard his jaw ached. His mind raced, screaming at him that there was no way this bastard was walking out of here. No one was.

But his brother, he had to get him help. Had to…

The masked man tilted his head, almost amused, his finger ghosting over the trigger.

"How about I make the choice for you?"

Time slowed.

The masked man's gun jerked toward its target…

BOOM! BOOM!

The deafening blasts tore through the air. Whiteboy didn't even realize he had pulled the trigger until he saw the masked man lurch back, the bodies falling backwards as the bullet tore into flesh. Blood sprayed the wall behind him in thick, dark splatters.

When he woke, it was to the distant hum of a television. The flickering light cast eerie shadows across the cluttered, shabby room.

His lips were dry. Throat raw. His body felt heavy, like he was sinking into whatever makeshift bed he had been placed on. For a second, disoriented, he fought to remember where he was and what happened.

Then it hit him. The car. The blood. The blackout. Instinctively, his hand shot to his side. Bandages. Fresh and wrapped tight. Someone had patched him up.

He tried to push himself up, but some small movement caught his attention. Across the room, standing in front of the small, static-filled TV, was a little girl. Her wide eyes locked onto him, unmoving. She clutched something in her hands, a worn-out doll, its stuffing peeking from the seams.

Before he could speak, a familiar voice came from the doorway.

"As-salamu alaikum, my brother."

Whiteboy turned his head slowly, and there he was, his Muslim brother from prison. Hakeem. Dressed simply in Muslim garbs, his presence was calm, almost reassuring.

But Whiteboy's paranoia wasn't letting up. His mind raced with questions.

How the hell did I get here?

To Be Continued…
IN The Streetz 6
Coming Soon

OTHER BOOKS BY

Urban Aint Dead

Tales 4rm Da Dale

The Hottest Summer Ever

Hittin' Licks For The Holidays: Atlanta

Wet Dreams On Lockdown: The Nurse

How To Publish A Book From Prison

How To Invest In The Stock Market From Prison

By **Elijah R. Freeman**

Despite The Odds

Despite The Odds 2

By **Juhnell Morgan**

Good Girls Gone Rogue

Good Girls Gone Rogue 2

By **Manny Black**

Hittaz

Hittaz 2

Hittaz 3

Hittaz 4

Hittaz 5

Hittaz 6

Coldhearted

Coldhearted 2

Coldhearted 3

By **Lou Garden Price, Sr.**

Charge It To The Game

Charge It To The Game 2

Charge It To The Game 3

A Summer To Remember With My Hitta

Snatched Up By A Hitta

Santa Sent Me A Real One For Christmas

Wet Dreams On Lockdown: The Unit Manager

Thug Me The Right Way 2

Thug Me The Right Way 3

Seizing A Gangsta's Heart For The Summer

Yours For The Taking

Wrapped Up In A Hitta's Love For Christmas

By **Nai**

A Set Up For Revenge

A Set Up For Revenge 2

Wet Dreams On Lockdown: The Librarian

By **Ashley Williams**

Trickin' On A Heaux For Christmas

Homie Hoppin' For The Holidays

Wet Dreams On Lockdown: The Female C.O

Letters Of His Love

By **Telia Teanna**

The State's Witness

The State's Witness 2

The State's Witness 3

This Time Won't You Save Me

This Time Won't You Save Me 2

His Summer Side Piece

A Holiday Heist

Healing The Heart Of A Detroit Gangsta

By **Kyiris Ashley**

Stuck In The Trenches

Stuck In The Trenches 2

By **Huff Tha Great**

Melted The Heart Of A Menace

Wet Dreams On Lockdown: Lieutenant Grace

By **P. Wise**

Merry Trapmas

By **Mia Sky**

Thug Me The Right Way

By **DiamondATL & Nai**

Wet Dreams On Lockdown: The Counselor

By **Paris Iman**

Wet Dreams On Lockdown: The Male C.O

By **Tamyra Griffin**

Wet Dreams On Lockdown: The Captain

By **TN Jones**

Wet Dreams On Lockdown: The Warden

By **Shawnice**

Atlantastan

Atlantastan 2

By **Chris Green**

IN The Streetz

IN The Streetz 2

IN The Streetz 3

IN The Streetz 4

By **Tron Hill**

Hittin' Licks For The Holidays: New York

By **Freshh Moneyy**

Coming Soon From
URBAN AINT DEAD

Drill
The Hottest Summer Ever 2
THE G-CODE
Tales 4rm Da Dale 2
How To Build Your Credit From Prison
By **Elijah R. Freeman**

Good Girls Gone Rogue 3
By **Manny Black**

Despite The Odds 3
By **Juhnell Morgan**

Wizdom: Forever Your Gangsta
By **Nai**

The Promissory
This Time Won't You Save Me 3
By **Kyiris Ashley**

Atlantastan 3
By **Chris Green**

IN The Streetz 6
By **Tron Hill**

Bandemic
By Freshh Moneyy

BOOKS BY
URBAN AINT DEAD's C.E.O

<u>Elijah R. Freeman</u>

Triggadale 1, 2 & 3

Tales 4rm Da Dale

The Hottest Summer Ever

Murda Was The Case 1, 2 & 3

Hittin' Licks For The Holidays: Atlanta

Wet Dreams On Lockdown: The Nurse

How To Publish A Book From Prison

How To Invest In The Stock Market From Prison

www.ingramcontent.com/pod-product-compliance
Lightning Source LLC
Chambersburg PA
CBHW071419300726
48976CB00004B/1176